The Genius
and
the Muse

Elizabeth Hunter

The Genius and the Muse
Copyright © 2012
by Elizabeth Hunter
ISBN: 1475119054

This is a work of fiction. Names, characters, places, and incidents are the products of the author's imagination, or are used fictitiously. Any resemblance to actual persons, living or dead, business establishments, events, or locales is entirely coincidental.

Cover Design: E. Hunter
Edited by: Amy Eye
Formatted by: Amy Eye

OTHER BOOKS BY ELIZABETH HUNTER

The Elemental Mysteries
A Hidden Fire
This Same Earth
The Force of Wind
A Fall of Water

For more information, please visit:
http://ElizabethHunterWrites.com

TO KELLI
FOR LOTS OF REASONS.

ACKNOWLEDGMENTS

Just prior to publication, my life took a turn that made this story even more personal than it already was. Life is unpredictable, to say the least. And I've found out just how amazing my friends and family are.

To my pre-readers, Kristy, Lindsay, Sarah, Sandra, Caroline, Molly, and Ron. How many times can I thank you before it starts to get weird?

To my friend, Lydia, who met me for dim sum and encouragement. Here's to taking things and running with them. You were an agent of change in my life.

A huge debt of gratitude to Toni Cox for her technical and artistic advice. Your insights were invaluable.

To my editor, Amy Eye. Thank you. Always, *thank you*.

To my readers all over the world, who I like to think are the best and brightest. Thank you for your patience and attention.

To my son, who makes living every day such an adventure.

And a special thank you to my amazing friend, Nicole, and her *sparks* of inspiration.

Here's to finding new dreams and rediscovering what you've lost.

Who sees the human face correctly? The photographer, the mirror, or the painter?

—PABLO PICASSO

Part One:
The Student

CHAPTER ONE

Foothill Art Institute
Claremont, California
March 2010

Kate Mitchell tripped over the ridge of cracked asphalt, the stumble sending her backpack falling to the ground, scattering notebooks, pencils, and a bag of lens caps and filters across the parking lot. Her camera bag started to slide. She caught it just before the padded case slipped off her arm.

"Perfect," she said as she glared at the backpack. Kate shoved her unruly red hair out of her eyes and set the carefully packed camera case with her SLR and lenses to the side before she began to pick up the rest of the scattered mess from her backpack. She could already feel the sweat starting to trickle between her thin shoulder blades as the Southern California sun radiated from the blacktop. "As if this day couldn't get any better…"

She had a sneaking suspicion that she'd forgotten to put sunscreen on again, and she prayed her pale, freckled skin wouldn't be red by the time she got inside. She finished tossing the last of her school supplies in her backpack and hustled toward the old building set in the foothills of the San Bernardino Mountains.

As she neared the sprawling building that housed the school of visual arts, she heard the clanging and ringing of hammers from the metal-fabrication shop just past the ceramic kilns, and the chatter from a group of splattered painters who were gathered by a bench near the entrance. Kate finally reached the cool shade of a spreading pepper tree, set her bags down, and tried to tame her hair into a bun before continuing on toward her first class.

Though it wasn't even April, the temperatures were already expected to be in the high 80s, and Kate was flushed by the time she reached the glass doors of the entrance. She felt her phone vibrating in her pocket and grabbed it to read a message from her boyfriend.

Call me when you finish class and meetings today. —Cody

Curious, she sent back a quick text.

What's up? —Kate

Pulling open the side door to the building, she sighed at the rush of cool, dry air that poured out.

What are your plans this weekend?—C

She walked down the wide hall toward the restroom to check her hair, which had probably already flown in eight different directions.

I have thesis work, and there's an exhibition I need to go to.—K

No one else was in the bathroom, so Kate took a moment to splash water on her red, freckled face. She patted her skin dry, pulled herself together, and hurried out, checking the screen on her phone to see if she had enough time to make a quick pass through the alumni gallery before her History of Photography class.

Deciding she could stop for ten minutes, Kate turned right instead of left and wandered down the long hall containing past student work from notable alumni of Foothill Art Institute.

Nope. You're going to San Diego with me and the guys.—C

She rolled her eyes.

That's news to me.—K

Kate walked through the gallery, scanning the walls for any new additions. Her work would be here one day. She'd already picked out the print she would submit to her advisor, Professor Bradley. She may not have been sure of other parts of her life, but when it came to photography, Kate knew exactly where she wanted to go.

Come on, babe. Take a break for once. Mom already booked a room for you.—C

"Damn it, Cody, some of us don't run surf shops," she said to her phone. She thought about Cody's mom and dad, whom she had loved since she was a little girl. The last thing she wanted to do was ruin a weekend that Barbara had planned. Their families had been close friends for years. Their mothers met when Kate and Cody were babies. They'd grown up together, and had been friends before they developed an undeniable chemistry together as teenagers. By the time college rolled around, it took no one by surprise when they started dating.

Cody had been her first boyfriend and the only man she'd seriously dated since graduating from high school. In the back of her mind, she knew their parents were both expecting marriage. But Kate had always been focused on her education and her photography, and no one seemed to question whether she was settling too quickly.

Until recently, she hadn't questioned it herself.

She glared at her phone and sent a quick text back.

I can't. I've got to get this done, Cody. I've got deadlines coming up.—K

Cody had been supportive and proud of her work as long as they'd been together. He'd been her unofficial assistant on a shoot more than once, especially if it was at the beach. Still, the closer she got to finishing her master's thesis and getting serious about developing her portfolio, the more Cody seemed to be dissatisfied with where she was headed.

Walking swiftly past the screen prints and paintings at the beginning of the gallery, Kate moved around the partitions to make her way to the back corner where photography prints from past students hung scattered on the walls.

She felt her phone buzz again.

Fine. Whatever. I guess I'll tell my mom you're not coming. Maybe Brad can invite his girlfriend.—C

Shaking her head, Kate continued on toward the center of the photography exhibit. She stopped and sat on the small bench, trying to quash her irritation with Cody so she could absorb the numerous images produced by Foothill Art Institute's most famous graduate, Reed O'Connor. With her back to the rest of the gallery, she studied the early work of one of her favorite photographers, who was also partly the subject of her graduate project.

Reed O'Connor had made his name quickly in the art world. Still in his early thirties, his dramatic good looks, mysterious personal life, and reclusive persona made him an intriguing and attractive subject for gossip. But his work, in Kate's opinion, was the real mystery.

Even as a student, the tell-tale characteristics of what would come to be known as an "O'Connor portrait" were evident. Along with an impressive technical prowess, the young photographer exhibited an almost impressionistic use of light and shadow and an artful isolation of features. It was a singular style he'd perfected in the eight years since he graduated from Foothill.

Kate leaned her thin arms against the back of the bench and scanned the collection of photographs.

O'Connor's portrait work was often controversial to the celebrities and other public figures who clamored for his attention, but the artist had managed to create a stunning mystique with his meteoric rise from fashion to portrait photography. His portrait work had appeared in leading magazines around the world. He was notoriously private, constantly in demand, and stubbornly single-minded. He used no assistants, she knew from her research, and he absolutely *never* captured the subject's full visage.

"Hey, Kate? Are you in here?"

She turned, hearing a familiar voice call from the entrance of the gallery. She smiled when Michelle, her friend and roommate from freshman year, walked around a corner. Kate lifted a hand in greeting.

"Hey." She scooted over to share the small bench. "How'd you know I was in here?"

"Where else are you before your first class on Thursday?" Michelle sat down beside her. "Still studying the enigmatic portrait?"

"Mmhmm," Kate said with a nod; then both girls fell silent as they stared toward the wall. "It's just so… not him."

"But it is him."

"But it's not."

Michelle huffed. "Whatever, photography geek. You're obsessed."

The picture that continued to fascinate Kate, even after years of contemplation, was a small 8x10 in the top right corner of the wall. It wasn't a typical "O'Connor portrait" for a number of reasons—though it might appear to be to someone less well-versed in his work. It had always caught her eye, despite the fact that it wasn't the most prominently displayed picture on the wall.

The light was unique. The lens, less sharply focused. Most importantly, instead of a singular focus for the camera's eye, the model was shown as if the photographer was looking over her right shoulder, and a man's hand was visible resting on it, as if he was trying to capture the girl or get her attention.

It was in soft black and white. The light spilled over the gentle curve of the girl's jaw, shadowing her neck and reflecting off the soft strands of hair, which waved behind her ear. Her head tilted as if the photographer had captured the image just before the subject turned her head, and the rise of the cheek hinted at a smile without showing one.

The man's hand rested on the shoulder, but the tips of the fingers curled, as if they were just about to grab hold. They were long and stained at the tips. Dark hair dusted the back of the hand and wrist. The nails were neat, but the skin was cracked near the cuticles. She'd always wondered if O'Connor was the owner of the hand and who the model was whom he'd captured with such uncharacteristic tenderness.

"Don't you have class at nine?"

Kate shrugged, still staring at the print on the wall.

"Kate?"

"Yeah?"

"Class, Kate." She felt Michelle shove her shoulder. "You know… the reason you've been coming here every day for six years?"

Finally, she shook her head and looked over at Michelle. "Yeah… class. What time is it?"

"About ten till. You should get going."

She grumbled and bent to pick up her backpack and camera bag. Tossing another look at the mystery portrait and hoisting her bags over her shoulder, she trudged toward the exit with Michelle.

"Hey!" Kate suddenly stopped, looking at her friend. "What are you doing in here? You don't have class on this floor, do you?"

"Oh!" Michelle's eyes lit up. "Professor Seever told me about some new sketches that someone cleaning out the painting studio found last month. They're by Rhodes, from when she was going here. Just anatomy studies, I guess, but she's notable enough now that they matted them and put them up. I was going to take a look."

Kate nodded toward the painting section. "Well, let's go. My class is right down the hall, so I still have a few minutes. Plus"— she grinned— "Bradley's teaching this one; he won't mind if I'm a little late."

"A little?" Michelle laughed. Heading toward the opposite side of the long, narrow gallery, the two girls approached a collection of paintings from various graduates, some still known and many others who had drifted into obscurity. In the middle of the far wall, between an abstract portrait in charcoal and a watercolor seascape in oils, hung three simple frames containing pen and ink studies. They were small, no more than eight by twelve inches, but had been matted so the notable signature of the artist was evident.

S. Rhodes.

The top sketch was a study of a man's arm and neck from the side. It was long and muscled, the definition particularly detailed along the neck and shoulder. The middle picture was a leg and foot. The thigh was lean and defined, its knee bent as if the model was lying down on a flat surface.

It was when Kate's eyes reached the bottom sketch that her breath caught in her throat. She stepped closer, her eyes riveted to the wall. Inside the plain matte was the study of a male hand—a very familiar hand. In fact, one glance told her that the long fingers, smooth calluses and slightly cracked cuticles of that hand belonged, without a doubt in her mind, to the same man who grasped the shoulder of the model in the mysterious O'Connor portrait.

She stared, transfixed by the same hand that she had studied from a different angle, in a unique work, done in an entirely separate medium on the other side of the gallery.

"Kate?"

"It's the same," she whispered. "It has to be. Who—"

"Kaitlyn?"

Her wide blue eyes finally left the frame to stare blankly at her friend.

"Huh?"

Michelle looked at her watch. "Class, Kate. You're going to be *really* late if you don't leave right now."

"Oh." She drew in a ragged breath. "Okay, thanks."

Michelle cocked her head and looked at her. "You all right?"

Kate nodded. "Uh-huh. Sure. We, uh… we better go."

Glancing back at the sketch, Kate turned and left the alumni gallery where the two hands, one drawn in pen and one captured by the lens, almost seemed to reach toward each other from opposite silent walls.

Part Two: The Professor

CHAPTER TWO

Foothill Art Institute
Claremont, California
March 2010

Kate gratefully slipped off her heavy backpack and dumped it beside her chair in Professor Christopher Bradley's empty office. Her camera bag was set carefully on the work table in the corner. She reached into her backpack to retrieve her graduate portfolio and the binder where she kept her notes for her thesis project on Reed O'Connor and twenty-first century interpretations of beauty. Finally, she leaned back and closed her eyes for moment, resting while she waited for her advisor.

She was almost dozing when she heard the door swing open and heavy footsteps enter the room. She kept her eyes closed, though she heard his chair squeak as he sat behind his desk.

"You know, Kate, if I can stay awake to teach that class when I have a three-month-old baby at home, you could at least make the effort to *appear* to be awake." His sardonic voice reached through the fog of her exhaustion as she finally opened her eyes.

She stared into the amused face of her graduate advisor. "Why were so you insistent I take this class, Professor Bradley?"

He narrowed his eyes. "Will you ever call me Chris? You call Dee by her first name, but you refuse to call me Chris. I really don't ask my grad students to be so formal."

"It just feels weird… Chris." Kate visibly grimaced when she said her professor's first name.

Chris Bradley and his wife Deepali were both Foothill graduates. He was a professor; she was a commercial photographer. Both were in their mid-thirties and would often invite graduate students over for meals on the weekends. Those evenings had been some of Kate's favorite memories of art school, and she knew that she would miss both Professor Bradley and Dee when she finished her thesis that summer.

Chris Bradley just laughed and shook his head. "You can call me Professor if you must. Even though it makes me feel old."

Kate gave him her best smart-ass grin. "You *are* old, Professor Bradley."

"You do remember I have control over your graduate requirements, right?" He narrowed his brown eyes. "I foresee the need for a new grad student to teach the Intro to Digital Photography seminar very soon. There's one coming up in a few weekends, in fact."

"*Young*, I mean. You're so young to be a professor here, Chris. Didn't you just graduate a few years ago?" She plastered an innocent smile on her face, and he couldn't help but smile. "Besides, I will be out of your clutches very soon, Professor Chris. You will have no power to inflict me on freshmen and retirees in a few months."

She may have called him "professor," but Chris Bradley was more friend than teacher to Kate, no matter how she addressed him. She knew his patient mentoring had taught her to be a better photographer. His passionate emphasis on the basic elements of photography had given her an appreciation and thorough knowledge of aspects she would have otherwise skimmed over in her enthusiasm for new techniques. In addition to that, Kate knew he and Dee had looked out for her personally, and she would always think of them as friends.

Nevertheless, Kate sighed. "Seriously, Prof—Chris, why are you making me take this history course? It's dead boring... despite your riveting presentation, of course."

"Oh, of course." He chuckled. "Pay attention, Kate. You can learn a lot from history. It informs everything we do as artists. Our vision is formed by our past."

"I thought our vision is what we want to see in the future."

"It's both, of course." He ran his fingers through messy brown hair and kicked his chair back. "Our history informs what steps we take toward the future. We can no sooner dismiss our past than we can dismiss the medium we choose to express ourselves through as artists."

Kate whispered, "Yes, Master Jedi."

He shook his head and smiled. "So young," he said. "You'll figure it out eventually."

"And moving along with the theme of 'figuring it out,' I have some questions for you on the aperture settings I was using in that canyon shoot. Can you take a look?"

The two photographers launched into a discussion of light and shadow, wrapped in the technical jargon of digital photography. Kate did all of her work in digital medium. She loved the freedom it gave her to manipulate images and experiment with different effects. In her opinion, it was also easier to process. Instead of spending hours in a darkroom peeling the skin off her hands with water and chemicals, she ruined her eyes with hours spent in front of a computer monitor. Art, she knew, would always take a toll, whether it was calluses or eye strain. Kate had picked eye strain.

They argued and debated back and forth for forty-five minutes as they studied her proofs. By the end of their appointment, Kate and Chris were both drained, and it was nearing lunch time.

Professor Bradley asked, "Want to join me? I packed leftovers from dinner last night."

Kate's eyes lit up. "Did Dee cook?"

"Of course. Why do you think I brought the leftovers? It's chicken biryani."

"Yes, please!" Kate grabbed her binder from the desk, inadvertently knocking over a picture on her professor's desk along with a half-empty coffee cup. "Oops, sorry. Let me help."

She quickly bent to her backpack to retrieve some napkins she'd stuffed there the day before. Turning back, she started to mop up the coffee as Chris did the same on his side. Luckily, he was a fairly organized teacher, so his desk wasn't littered with anything other than lens caps and a few filters.

Kate picked up the picture she'd knocked over, turning it to wipe off the front where it had fallen in the spill. It was a color snapshot of a group of young people sitting on the porch of an old log cabin she'd never really noticed before. Looking more closely, she realized she recognized some of the people in the picture.

She grinned. "Is this you and Dee?"

Chris glanced up to see her holding the frame. A small smile lifted the corner of his mouth. "Yes, we were still in school.

Maybe… seven or eight years ago? We must have been about your age when that was taken."

Kate smiled and looked over the young faces in the picture. There was Dee and Chris. A tall African-American woman who looked vaguely familiar and a laughing blonde with messy hair. Sitting beside her professor and his wife was one other couple with their arms wrapped around each other.

"Is that—" Kate paused and squinted, unsure of who she thought she was seeing. "Is that Reed O'Connor with you?"

O'Connor's piercing blue gaze stared into the lens. Kate hadn't known he had blue eyes. He was rarely photographed in public, and when he was, he always wore dark glasses.

"Yes, that's Reed. I thought you knew we went to school together. We graduated the same year, in fact."

Kate had never seen a picture of him from his past, even though she'd looked through old yearbooks in the library. The few pictures of the photographer she'd seen had all been taken in the last few years, since his photography had become nationally known. And he was always alone. Even in group pictures, he seemed to hold himself separate.

She looked again. O'Connor's dark hair was longer in the snapshot and curled a little as it fell around his ears. A messy dusting of stubble was visible on his jaw. Though he wasn't smiling, there was a slight smirk at the corner of his mouth as if he was restraining himself from breaking into laughter at whoever was holding the camera.

She shook her head. "You know, I never really thought about it. You look like you were friends." Kate narrowed her gaze at her advisor. "Why didn't you tell me?"

"We… uh, we were friendly." Chris chuckled. "But I wouldn't call us friends. He and Dee were friends. Though he did steal my girlfriend once."

Kate's mouth gaped in shock and she looked back at the picture. "What? But Dee—you're with Dee here." She stopped and frowned. "I'm confused."

Chris just laughed. "It's not what you're thinking, and 'girlfriend' is an exaggeration." He paused. "I'm not talking about me and Dee. I'm talking about Sam, the blonde." He nodded toward the picture in her hand, and Kate looked again.

"She and I only went out a few times. Sam and Dee were roommates; that's how we met. Honestly, I had a bit of a thing for Dee as soon as Sam introduced us. And then, when Sam met

Reed... Well, it all worked out for the best. Sam was nuts about Reed, and I was nuts about Dee. I may have played up my heartbreak a little bit for sympathy, but I was actually pretty happy." He winked at her shocked expression.

"Dee fell for that?"

"I tried my hardest to seem heartbroken and in need of comfort, but I'm pretty sure she saw through it."

"So, who is this in the picture with O'Connor? Her name was Sam?" Kate cocked her head and studied it. "She looks... kind of familiar, now that I think about it."

"Sam's a nickname. I'm sure you've heard of her. She's pretty well known in Southern California. A painter. Still works around here. Her professional name is Samantha Rhodes."

"S. Rhodes." Kate gasped in realization. "The hand..."

The hand that Sam Rhodes has sketched so many years before. The same hand in the mysterious O'Connor portrait. She looked between the photographer and the painter in the picture. The hand in the sketch and the photograph belonged to O'Connor. It had to. Was the woman in the photograph this painter? Kate couldn't tell from the photograph, but suddenly she felt a spark of curiosity start to burn.

Chris leaned forward. "Hand? What hand?"

She shook her head. "Nothing. So they dated, huh? O'Connor and this painter?"

"Oh, yes. They were together for... about six years, I think. And they were magnetic, the two of them. So much talent. They just drew people around them. Dee's the one that introduced them; she and Reed knew each other from when they were kids."

"Wasn't that weird?" Kate cocked an eyebrow. "I mean, when you broke up? Also, how did I not know that Dee was friends with the guy I'm writing about for my thesis?"

Chris shrugged. "It wasn't, really. Sam and I were never serious. Nothing like she and Reed were. And he's very private. Dee respects that. She doesn't talk about their friendship much outside of our group of friends."

"The people here?"

"Yes, that's me and Dee, of course. Vanessa Allensworth, the painter. And... that's Susan beside her." Chris laughed. "I think she'd just finished firing the kiln they had at the cabin. She's a potter. And then Sam and Reed, of course. So, yeah, that's most of us."

"Wow." Kate frowned. "That's so unexpected."

"What part?" he laughed. "That I had friends or that I dated someone other than my wife?"

"No, not that!" She blushed, finally setting the picture down, though she faced it toward her on the desk so she could study it. "You never read about Reed O'Connor being involved with anyone. Or even friendly with anyone. He's like this photographic mystery man. He kind of comes across as a hermit."

Chris folded his arms across his chest. "Reed is... He had a lot of people he was friendly with, though not too many I'd say he really called friends. He was always pretty aloof except with a few people. He's very fond of Dee. I know they still keep in contact. He's close friends with Javier Lugo, the sculptor. Javi's the one who took that picture, actually. And then... well, Sam was on another level entirely."

Kate tore her eyes from O'Connor to examine the blond woman in the photograph, studying her dark eyes and open smile. She had dramatic features that wouldn't be considered classically beautiful, but would probably photograph well. Her nose was a bit too long for her face, and her jaw was strong. She looked joyful and bursting with life, in complete contrast to the solemn man behind her. She sat on the steps in front of the cabin, and the lanky photographer sat behind her. She smiled as she leaned into him. Her head tilted in his direction, though her eyes stayed on the camera, and O'Connor's legs stretched out on either side of her as his head dipped toward hers.

The two artists were both eye-catching, a study in contrasts. O'Connor's hair was almost black, hers was a rich gold. His eyes were a vivid blue, and hers were a warm brown. Even their skin contrasted as they twisted their limbs together, and her warm sun-kissed tan glowed against his pale arms. Despite all that, the two seemed to meld together. Their arms and legs twisted in a way that made it hard to tell where he ended and she began.

"They're gorgeous," Kate murmured.

She caught her professor's curious look out of the corner of her eye. "They were. Like I said, they were magnetic. Both of them were so brilliant. Very talented. They were... each other's muse, I think."

"Really?" She frowned. "I've never heard of O'Connor using one model exclusively. Or even habitually."

"That's not exactly what I mean. Partly, but not exactly." He paused before he continued. "I think, Kate, if you *really* want to understand Reed O'Connor, you have to understand Samantha Rhodes."

She narrowed her eyes. "What are you saying?"

Chris smiled and offered an enigmatic shrug. "I'm saying you can learn a lot from history."

CHAPTER THREE

Claremont, California
March 2000

"Could someone tell whatever large person who is standing behind me to get the hell out of my light?"

The tall shadow didn't move, but stayed, hovering behind her as she tried to smooth the sepia oil with her pinky finger. Annoyed, Sam finished the last sweep of the tree trunk she was working on and turned to glance over her shoulder. Meeting only a broad male chest covered by a Blink 182 concert shirt, she lifted her gaze to a pair of intense blue eyes and a cocky smirk.

"Beautiful," he said.

"Really? There'd be more of it to like if you would move your ass out of my light."

"I wasn't talking about the painting."

Sam rolled her eyes. "Does that line actually work for you?"

The stranger stuck his hand out. "I'm Reed O'Connor, Deepali's friend."

Sam looked at his hand, but left it there hanging as she wiped her hands absent-mindedly on a dirty rag.

"I figured. Is Dee back already? I didn't hear her come in." Sam looked around the man's shoulders toward the door, which was hanging open. Their whole building had a fairly open-door policy, but usually, only residents roamed the halls.

She squinted up at the tall man. "Did someone let you in?"

"I just came from downstairs. I crashed at my friend's place last night; I'm stumbling up here now. Javier Lugo. Short guy. Grumpy, doesn't talk much? He moved in a couple of weeks ago."

She nodded and tried unsuccessfully to scrape the paint from under her fingernails. "Huh. Sculptor, right? Metals? Is he a mechanic, too? That's a nice apartment, by the way. His name's Javier?"

"He's kind of all three. And call him Javi; he hates Javier. And I'm Reed. Like I said. Why didn't you and Dee move into that place when it was empty? This building doesn't have an elevator."

She continued to measure him with a slight frown as she cleaned up around her easel. Sam finally pointed toward the large skylights that covered the ceiling. "Light."

"Ah." He nodded.

She moved toward the small corner kitchen to get a drink of water and drop her brushes in the old soup cans filled with turpentine that lined the back of the counter. "So you just moved to town? And you're going to Foothill, right? What are you studying? You and Dee grew up together?"

"Sort of," he replied vaguely. "And yeah, I'm studying photography. When is she going to be back?"

Sam didn't answer, but grabbed a glass from the counter and filled it, taking a long drink and glancing at the man who had settled on the small couch. Between Sam's art equipment and Dee's camera gear spread everywhere, the actual living area was pretty small, and Reed more than filled it with his presence.

She narrowed her eyes, measuring him. Dee said he was good-looking, and she wasn't exaggerating. If anything, she'd understated it. Reed O'Connor could have been a model. Sam guessed by the stretch of clothes over his body that he'd look pretty perfect without them. She squinted, mentally undressing him and posing him in different configurations.

"You know, if you want to just hop in bed, I'm perfectly okay with that."

Sam looked at Reed, and her lip curled a little. "What?"

"Well, you're kind of looking at me like you're imagining me naked. So I thought you might be, well…" He grinned at her from the couch. "Imagining me naked."

She continued frowning at him. "I *was* imagining you naked."

"No use wasting time, then. Where's your bedroom?"

Understanding finally broke through, and Sam scowled as she threw the paint-smudged rag at him. "Pervert. I want to sketch you. That's why I'm imagining you naked."

He shrugged. "No problem. You can sketch me post-coitally any time you like."

"Excuse me?" Her eyebrows shot up.

"Of course, you might be too exhausted after…" Reed trailed off with a thoughtful look. "Want to do it before? That could be a real turn on, if you think about it." He stretched out his long legs and posed. "*Very* extended foreplay. I like it. Fine. I'll extend the sketching invitation to pre-coital nudity as well. Is pre-coital a word?"

"Wow. Dee wasn't exaggerating about that part."

His eyebrows shot up. "What? What part? Dee and I haven't ever… you know." Reed made an obscene hand gesture as Sam rolled her eyes. "Strictly friends. Anything else would be weird. But I'm glad to know my reputation precedes me."

"No, she begged me not to kill you before she got back. She also begged me not to move out, since apparently you're going to be around more," Sam muttered, staring at him as he stretched out on the couch.

Reed frowned. "Oh, well that's not nearly as flattering. I *am* very good in bed, though, if you wanted to do a more careful study. For artistic purposes, of course."

His arms were long, but he was well-proportioned and his coloring was dramatic. If she painted him in color, would a neutral work best behind him? Maybe blue to compliment his eyes? She traced the length of his legs and wondered just how proportional he was before she caught herself.

"I definitely want to paint you," Sam said.

"Getting messy with paint has definite possibilities, too; though the clean-up is something to consider."

She shook her head. "Are you always like this?"

He gave a small, but surprisingly sincere, smile. "Honestly? No. Mostly I'm a moody asshole. But I just finished a big project, slept really well last night—which is unusual for me—and I'm really looking forward to seeing Dee, so this is me in a good mood."

"You're in some kind of mood, all right," she said under her breath. Her old-fashioned upbringing finally kicked in when she realized she hadn't offered her guest anything to drink. "You want some water or something?" She took a long gulp from her own glass.

He chuckled. "Are you always so polite?"

She felt a small, inadvertent smile try to make an appearance, but she shoved it back. "No, usually I'm much more polite to company, but I forgot you were coming to meet Dee, and I got started working on something. Plus, you've hit me with at least three pick-up lines since walking through the door."

"I think it might have been four."

"It's impressive in an obnoxious way, I guess."

He looked over his shoulder at the painting she had been working on. "Do you usually do landscapes? You're good at them. I like the way you used the light in that one."

Sam was working on a painting of an old cabin surrounded by soaring pine trees, set on the edge of a lake. The front of the cabin was shaded by an old porch, and a wooden dock stretched out into the water. A small boat bobbed in the foreground.

She answered as her eyes examined the painting from across the room. "No, not usually. I'm more interested in people. But I got an assignment to do a landscape in oils, so I decided to paint my grandfather's cabin."

"I'm sure he'll love it."

She shrugged. "He's dead, so I kinda doubt he'll care. My parents still live around there. They'll like it."

Sam caught him studying her out of the corner of her eye. "Oils are a good medium for you."

She snorted. "Hardly. They take too much time. And I hate the smell. I like watercolors some, but acrylics are what I prefer."

"I don't actually know that much about painting. I sketch some."

"Post-coitally?"

Reed grinned. "Of course."

Hearing a commotion in the stairwell, they turned toward the sound of labored footsteps trudging toward the apartment. Deepali Mehra, loaded down with camera equipment, panted as she made it to the door of the third floor walkup. She took a moment to glare at Samantha.

"Light, my ass! Why are you my roommate, again?"

Sam shrugged and rinsed her glass out to set it in the strainer on the counter.

Reed jumped up and stepped over the coffee table. Dee spotted him. "Goliath!"

"You look like a miniature pack-mule, Deedee."

The tiny woman puffed, her face red from exertion. "I missed you too. Well, I missed your strong back and ability to carry all my shit, anyway."

He grinned at her, snickering as he helped her situate her tripod and camera case. When she was finally free of her equipment, Reed enfolded her in a long hug. Sam watched the friends as they whispered back and forth, laughing quietly as they shared some inside joke. She tore her eyes away to mix a pitcher of lemonade. Her roommate finally wandered into the kitchen with Reed trailing behind her.

"So, Sam, you and Reed haven't killed each other yet. This bodes well." Her voice was dripping with amusement.

Sam winked. "Give it time, Dee. He just got here." She finished filling the pitcher. "Plus, he says this is him in a good mood."

She stirred the lemonade and set it in the old fridge before she walked toward the door to grab her keys, purse and sunglasses. She looked down, absently noticing the paint splattered on her shirt and jeans. Whatever. She didn't feel like changing.

"I'm meeting Chris for lunch, so I'll be back later this afternoon. Reed... " Sam trailed off, at a loss for something to say.

"It was a pleasure," he said, smiling at her.

She smiled back. "It was something, all right. See you later."

Sam walked out, but before she could run down the stairs, she heard Reed say, "I think she likes me."

CHAPTER FOUR

Laguna Beach, California
March 2010

"Come on, babe, you have to come with us."

Kate sighed and looked at her boyfriend's adorable, pleading face. "I'd love to go, but I've got to finish this part of my thesis, Cody! Plus, there's an exhibition of O'Connor's work—"

"Not this shit again." He rolled his eyes at her. "When are you going to be done with all that stuff, Kate? You've put so many hours into that project already, and you totally don't have to. Didn't your advisor say you had enough for your degree already? You're doing *extra* work. Plus, you could get paying jobs right now. That guy from the magazine called the shop again last week asking about you, and—"

"I told him before, I'm not interested. I don't want to be taking pictures of surf competitions and doing family portraits as a career."

He looked at her cautiously. "So, what? That stuff's not good enough for you now? You've been photographing competitions for years. It was good enough to pay the bills in school, but not anymore? I thought that's what photographers did."

"It's not that. You know I'm going to keep taking pictures for the shop, and you guys—and I'll always do portraits for family. I just… if I went on staff full-time for that magazine, that would be all I'd have time for. And I think I have a lot more to say with my photography on an artistic level."

He shook his head and went back to sanding the board he was working on. "Whatever."

"Plus, I'd be traveling a lot with that job. Do you want me out of the country that much? We hardly ever see each other as it is."

He shrugged. "I guess."

She stared at him for a few minutes, lulled into relaxation by the repetitive shush of his sanding and the hum of traffic along the Pacific Coast Highway. Searching for a change of subject—something they wouldn't fight about—she remembered what she wanted to ask him.

"Professor Bradley and Dee invited us for dinner next week. Do you want to go?"

"Are you three going to be talking about your art and making me feel like an idiot again?" he asked, continuing to work the sander up and down the longboard.

"Cody—"

"Just tell me what day. I'll see if I can get away."

Kate stared at his sullen expression. "Okay, I'll ask and give you a call."

"Okay." Cody glanced at her. "I really need to finish this board up, babe."

Kate watched him quietly for a few more minutes before she got up and left the dusty work room, waving at one of his partners, who was surrounded by the typical gathering of beach bunnies that had wandered in from trolling the beach.

She walked out of the surf shop and into the bright sun of Laguna Beach. Kate realized she had forgotten to put on sunscreen that morning, so she couldn't walk along the water like she'd originally planned. With her pale, freckled skin—courtesy of her very Irish mother—she always fried within minutes.

Kate could hear the laughter of the beach volleyball players in the distance and the sound of children laughing on the playground. Everything about the scene was achingly familiar and yet, she still felt out of place. She blinked in the bright light, turned, and walked to her car.

Part Three:
The Photographer

CHAPTER FIVE

Claremont, California
March 2010

A week after the meeting with Chris, Kate leaned back in her chair and stretched after a home-cooked meal shared at the Bradley's table. She smiled at the small, dark-haired woman across from her and rubbed her tummy like a satisfied bear.

"So good. I'll never be able to cook like that."

"That's because you have no desire to."

"That's… completely true."

Deepali Mehra-Bradley smiled at Kate and leaned into her elbows on the table. Chris had taken baby Sabina upstairs to feed her and put her to bed, leaving the two women at the table to linger over coffee and talk.

"I love having you over, Kate. I'm going to miss you so much when you graduate. You're Chris's favorite student, you know. He's probably not supposed to have one, but I know you are." Dee smiled at her. "Do you and Cody have plans to move? Where is he tonight, by the way? I thought you would bring him."

She shrugged. "He's meeting the guys to talk about some promotion for the shop. I'm not sure. He knew I wanted to talk to you about O'Connor, and he's sick of the whole topic, so he begged off."

"No apologies needed. I remember Chris when he was doing his master's thesis on Adams. If I *never* heard another word about the revolutionary development of the Zone System, I would have been a happy, happy woman." Dee rolled her eyes, but smiled fondly at the memory.

"Is it nice, though, to be with another photographer? Sometimes I wish Cody had more interest in what I do." Kate propped her chin on her hand as she studied the woman who had come to feel very much like a trusted friend over the previous years.

Dee cocked her head and thought before answering. "It has its good points and bad, I suppose. There's a level of understanding when you're married to another artist. Chris understands when I get in a creative mood and want to lock myself away and work, because he feels the same way sometimes. It's harder when you have a family. Since the baby has come, we've had to temper those impulses, so we don't let each other get overwhelmed taking care of Sabina. I think he's better at that than I am. I still get much more obsessive about things."

"See, I don't think Cody really gets that." Kate shook her head. "Sometimes I'll be working on a project, and he'll want to do something and want me to just stop and drop everything. He doesn't understand why I can't take a break and pick it up later."

"But that's balance too, Kate. There's value in that, because life isn't always going to be about you and your art. It can easily become your whole life, and some artists choose to live like that, but you'll end up missing out on a lot. In the end, I think your photography would suffer for not living a full life."

Kate mulled over what the other woman had said before she spoke again. "How much time do you have now, for your non-work stuff?"

"What, the stuff that *doesn't* pay the bills?" Deepali laughed. "Not as much, of course. Between the commercial aspect of my business and then having Sabina, it's not as much. But… it's important to remember that this is just a season of my life, too. I'll always be a photographer, but my daughter won't always be small and need me to take care of her like I do now. In fact, according to my grandmother, I'm going to blink one day, and she'll be a grown woman." Her dark eyes danced with laughter.

"Your grandmother sounds like a wise woman."

"Yes, she is. I'm named after her, you know? I became 'Dee' later. In fact, Sam Rhodes gave me that nickname. Did Chris tell you? She's the first person that ever called me 'Dee.' I never had a nickname before that. Well, Reed called me 'Deedee' sometimes, but only to tease me when we were young. Sam though…" Dee started laughing. "When we first moved in together, she warned me that she would get in moods when she painted, and she only communicated in monosyllables, so I needed a one syllable nickname because Deepali was too long."

Kate smiled. "She sounds like she had a great sense of humor."

"She did—still does, though we don't talk as much now. I think…"

"What?" Kate leaned forward in her chair.

Dee just smiled enigmatically. "You know, I introduced Sam and Reed. He and I grew up together."

"I didn't know you were so close, or I probably would have bugged you about him before. And weren't you born in India? How did you and Reed grow up together?" Kate's eyebrows knit together.

Dee took a breath as if to speak, but then paused. "You know, that story is sort of his to tell. It's nothing dramatic, but he's a very private person. I hope you don't mind if I don't share that."

"Of course." Kate squashed the feeling of disappointment. "Do you still talk with him regularly?"

"Oh, I don't know if he talks with *anyone* regularly, except maybe Lydia, his agent. We still e-mail occasionally. He was always like that, though. I'd go for years without seeing him or even hearing from him. Then he'd drop back into my life, and it was like we'd never been apart."

"Were you two ever involved?"

Deepali belly laughed. "Oh, God, no! Oh, no no no. Reed— well, for one, he was almost like a brother to me. Also, he was just too—too big." She broke into laughter again when she saw Kate's face flush. "No, I don't mean like *that*!"

Her laughter died down a little before she spoke again. "He was overwhelming, Kate, especially when he was younger. His talent, his energy, his personality. I'm a pretty laid-back person. I think that's one of the reasons Chris and I are so good together. We're both very giving. He's a very thoughtful man. If I was with someone like Reed—no." Dee shook her head. "I would just disappear in the relationship. Eventually, it would have been all him. No me left."

"What about Samantha Rhodes?"

Dee's eye glowed. "Oh, Sam got Reed. From the beginning, even before they were really together."

"What do you mean, she 'got' him?"

Dee paused before she continued. "She understood him. I think in a way that no one else ever did. And he understood her." Her voice softened and a wistful look came into her eyes as she remembered. "They were a lot alike, in some ways. But different, too. Different enough that they could be together." Dee took a deep breath and Kate could see her energy quiver at the rush of memories. "They had this way about them when they were in the same room. Reed and I could be working on something for a class or a project, and we worked very well together. But if Sam was there—especially if she was working—it was like his energy just flowed. But then it focused, too. Like they fed off of each other, but instead of draining the other person, it just built and built until it spilled over. It was almost like a contact high. Anyone that spent time around them would tell you the same thing."

Kate watched Dee gaze off into the distance, her eyes lit with memories.

"I can't really imagine that. It must have been extraordinary."

Dee looked back at her. "It was. I've never felt anything like it since. Some of my best work was done after spending time with them. You could ask any of us that lived in the building. We all noticed it when we were around them. Chris, Javi, Vanessa, Susan. Even Lydia noticed it, and she wasn't even an artist."

"How—I mean, what happened to them? Chris said they broke up. How long were they together?"

Dee took another deep breath, her gaze narrowing as she thought. "They must have been together... six years, I think? The last year and a half of school, and then Sam went to New York with Reed after we all graduated. They were there for four years, I think. They broke up, and then she moved back to her family home to work. She's not that far from here, just up in the mountains on one of the lakes."

"Do you know what happened? Why did they break up?"

Dee's eyes were guarded. "Not firsthand. I've heard bits and pieces from mutual friends, but I don't know the whole story. And, like I said before, that's not really my story to tell."

"Of course."

Dee took another sip of coffee, still lost in thoughts of the past.

"Did they ever model for each other?"

Deepali smiled. "Oh, yes. They modeled for each other. Sam had sketchbooks full of him. And Reed?" Dee snorted. "Well, Sam told me once she didn't know what was a more familiar sight, Reed's cock or his lens." Kate felt her face flush as Dee burst into laughter. She finally calmed down a bit. "Yes, Kate, they modeled for each other. But never together! And they were so beautiful together. His dark and her fair. Just gorgeous. Sad that there's not more pictures of them."

"I saw the picture in Chris's office."

"That old snapshot?" Dee smiled at Kate with a twinkle in her eye. "Javi took that. That's nothing. Here, come look. I've got a better one."

She rose, and Kate followed her into the studio at the back of the house. There was a small darkroom in the back corner, and the walls were lined with shelves stacked with all the equipment two working photographers could collect. Dee walked to a stack of filing cabinets.

"I don't have a print, but I took a beautiful picture of them once. One of my best portraits. I had to sneak up on them. Reed hated getting his picture taken. *Hated* it. So you always had to sneak up on him. I have the slide here… somewhere." She rifled through her files at the back of one cabinet until she held up a slide page in triumph. "Aha!"

Dee moved to one of the light boxes in the room and flipped it on. She retrieved a magnifying loupe and handed it to Kate. Moving to the side so she could look at it, a sad expression flickered across her face. "There they are."

Kate leaned down to peek at the small picture. It must have been a candid shot; neither of them was looking at the lens. Sam was sitting on Reed's lap facing him, with her legs wrapped around his waist and her arms around his back. His long legs stretched out on the grass, and he leaned toward her as if to kiss her.

He held her close, and his large hands, the hands from the photograph in the gallery, tangled in her hair as he drew her head toward his. Their bodies were pressed together, and their lips were only a whisper apart, but it was their eyes, which were locked on each other with a look of complete and total mutual adoration, that Kate couldn't stop staring at.

She stared at the slide, hardly noticing the tears that had come to her eyes. "So beautiful," she whispered. "So…" She trailed off, unable to describe the feeling that the photograph evoked. Passion. Possession. Kate couldn't say why the picture of the couple touched her so deeply, but when she saw it, she could almost feel their sense of complete and utter belonging.

"They were," Deepali said quietly, finally turning off the light box as Kate stepped away from it.

"Did you ever show them the picture?"

She nodded. "I gave a print to each of them. I never used it for anything. It's too personal. I never even made a copy for myself."

"I wonder…"

What had happened to them?

The spark of Kate's academic curiosity suddenly flared into something much more personal.

Dee wiped her eyes a little and cleared her throat. "Yeah, I think we all do."

CHAPTER SIX

Claremont, California
April 2000

"Oh shit!"

Sam looked up from her sketchbook, somewhat shocked at her roommate's sudden outburst. Dee had fallen asleep on the couch after another all-day session working with Reed. They were helping each other with their portfolios for a studio class, and the deadline for turning them in was fast approaching.

"What's wrong?"

"I forgot to send those slide pages home with Reed, and he needs them first thing in the morning for Professor Simon. Oh, I'm so exhausted." Dee groaned as she sat up, rubbing her eyes and grimacing.

"He absolutely has to have them? Come on, it's almost midnight," Sam said, trying to turn back to her sketchbook.

"Yeah, he lent them to me as a favor, and I forgot to give them back. Ugh, I better go and slip them under his door. He's meeting with Simon first thing in the morning."

Sam sighed. She didn't give a rat's ass about Reed O'Connor, but she did care about Dee, who was obviously exhausted. She had taken a nap that afternoon, so she'd planned to work late anyway. She stood and held out her hand.

"Here. Give 'em to me. I'll walk over to his place and slide them under the door. You need some sleep."

"Oh no, Sam. Seriously, he might be awake, and I don't want you guys bitching at each other because of my forgetfulness. I'll do it; just give me a minute."

"Sit. Or actually, go to bed. I'll do it, and I promise I won't bitch at him. It's practically midnight, he'll probably be sleeping. And if he's not, I promise I'll be civil."

Dee gave her an incredulous look, but handed over the clear slide pages she dug out of her backpack, then stumbled toward her bedroom. "Thanks, Sam. You're the best," she called out over her shoulder, smothering a yawn.

Sam tucked the slides in her messenger bag, threw a light sweater over her pajamas, and grabbed her keys as she walked out the door. Reed only lived a couple of blocks away, so she decided to walk instead of taking her old pick-up truck to the photographer's apartment.

She would have liked to say she was annoyed by Reed's almost constant presence in the apartment over the last month, but as much as he irritated her personally, Sam couldn't deny how talented the man was. He also seemed to bring out the best in Dee, so she had enjoyed watching her roommate bloom creatively.

Sam could even grudgingly admit the energy that flowed through the small apartment seemed to be benefiting her as well. She would never admit it to him, but Reed's presence stimulated her in more than one way. She had done some of her best work when she was in the same room with him. She couldn't explain it, because he was usually a complete asshole to everyone except Dee and his friend, Javi. The few times Chris had stopped by, Reed had curled only his lip at him, despite how nice Chris always was to Dee.

In fact, thinking about Chris and Dee, Sam was beginning to think someone was dating the wrong roommate. Chris was a nice guy. Their conversations were pleasant, and they had a lot of common interests. Still, Sam had a feeling a "better off as friends" conversation was fast approaching.

When she reached Reed's building, she looked up to his second floor apartment, where a window faced the quiet street. There wasn't a light on, but she did notice the window was open, and the thin curtain drifted outside, fluttering in the breeze that swept through the foothills that night. The moon was full and huge as it hung over the mountains and lit up the silent street.

She stepped into the apartment building. The door looked like it had been broken for a while, and she remembered Reed saying the residents kept their doors locked. She walked up the stairs, intending to slip the slides under the door as quickly as possible and make her way home. But as she reached his closed door, Sam could hear Reed talking in his apartment.

"No, no, no!" His low voice rumbled through the thin walls.

She knocked, curious what had made the man sound so distraught. She hoped he wasn't worried about the slides. It was just Professor Simon. After the sound of quiet shuffling, she heard his heavy footsteps approach the door. He opened it in a rush, and she saw him for the first time without a shirt.

Damn. He really was as perfect as she thought he'd be naked —well, almost naked.

Her gaze lingered on his chest. His abdomen was lightly defined, and a thin line of dark hair trailed down the center of his stomach toward jeans that hung loose on his hips. She glanced down. The muscles around his waist were clearly defined, and he was barefoot.

When she finally looked up again, Sam saw his eyes rake over her face as she examined him. In a heartbeat, he grabbed her hand and pulled her into the apartment, shutting the door behind her.

Reed pulled her into his arms and leaned down, swiftly laying his lips on hers in a consuming kiss. One hand spanned the small of her back, and the other threaded through her hair, tilting her face up as his mouth covered hers.

She froze, stunned by his sudden move, her temperature soaring as his lips moved against her own. She felt, rather than heard, the whimper escape her throat. Reed's stubble scraped against her skin, and she returned the kiss instinctively. Her hands lifted to his shoulders, clutching them as he pulled her closer. He kissed her without any hesitation, as if somehow, they had been lovers before.

Sam finally pulled away, gasping for air. He stared at her, his eyes fevered and needy.

"Am I dreaming?"

"No."

She stood motionless in the circle of his arms.

"Fuck."

Their eyes were still locked.

"Reed—"

"Take your clothes off. I need you in my bed." His words tumbled out in a rush as he stepped back and gestured toward the far corner of the room.

Sam's mouth dropped open. "What?"

He pulled the messenger bag off her shoulder and pushed her toward the unmade bed across the room. The sheets were rumpled as if he had been tossing and turning in his sleep.

"The light. Look at the light, Sam." He mumbled as he pointed toward the small bed. "The moon coming right through the window. Look at the shadows. It's so bright. It's perfect. I just need —fuck! I need someone in the bed. A nude. Where's that lens? Shit..." Reed trailed off, still muttering under his breath as he pulled camera bags apart looking for something and shoving back the dark hair that spilled into his eyes.

Understanding dawned when she looked at the bed and the moonlight streaming through the open window. It was so bright it cast crisp shadows on the rumpled white sheets, which seemed to glow in the night.

He needed a model to photograph. She nodded. Sam could understand that, though she was still stunned by his sudden kiss at the door and confused why he thought he had been dreaming.

"Will you sit for me?" Sam looked up when she heard his voice, plaintive in the corner of the room. His expression was almost manic as he waited for her response.

"You need a model," Sam finally said, as he walked toward her with his SLR and a lens in his hand.

He nodded, bending down at the table to affix the lens to the camera.

"Just a model?"

"Yes! Will you do it?"

"Okay. Sure, I guess. But that's it."

Samantha had modeled nude for both art classes and friends on numerous occasions. She wasn't especially modest, but she did need to make sure she and Reed were on the same page as far as expectations went. It wasn't like he'd been very secretive about his interest.

"Fine. Of course." He waved her toward the bed. She shrugged and moved over to get undressed. She had to admit, the light *was* gorgeous and abnormally bright. She completely understood why he wanted to capture it.

"You haven't been wearing any tight clothes today, have you?"

"No, there shouldn't be any lines—oh, maybe from my panties."

He waved absently as he took some test shots of the bed. "That's fine, we'll work around it. Nothing around your breasts?"

"No, I was in PJs most of the afternoon, actually. I just threw on shoes and a sweater to come over here."

"Tan lines?"

"Summer hasn't started, so that shouldn't be a problem."

"Perfect." His gaze lingered on her for a few moments as she undressed, but she quickly slipped under the thin sheet, and he bent down to move her arms and legs where he wanted to drape the material to cover her.

Sam inhaled sharply at the feel of his callused fingers on her skin. Though she had modeled before, the heated kiss they'd shared was throwing her off her usually remote modeling demeanor.

Reed finally reached up toward her head lying on his pillow and slowly pulled the tie from her hair. Sam had forgotten she'd put it up earlier, and she couldn't help but hold her breath as he gently tugged long sections over her shoulders to trail along the swell of her left breast. His own breath caught as his fingers hovered over her. His eyes met hers, and she could feel the energy snap as they stared at each other.

"Comfortable enough?" he whispered hoarsely.

She nodded and relaxed back into his pillow as he moved toward the table where he had set his camera. He stared at her, lying in his bed as if she had just woken from a dream in the moonlight. He swallowed visibly and began to work.

Sam lay frozen in place, her body utterly still as her mind raced. She was surrounded by his scent as she lay swathed in the sheets—soap, the faint scent of the aftershave he sometimes wore, and a trace of developer fluid. Her eyes followed him as he murmured instructions to her and moved around the room, completely focused on her body and the light. He reached over occasionally, adjusting an arm, a piece of hair, or the drape of the sheet. Every time Reed's fingers brushed her, they raised goosebumps. She was utterly aware of every small movement he made and each click of the camera as he captured her in the quickly shifting light. His eyes were so focused, Sam felt as if she could burst into flames at any moment.

He was hypnotic.

After what was probably an hour, Reed began to slow, and it was as if the energy drained from the room. He came and knelt beside her, setting his camera on the floor by his feet. His hand reached over, pulling the sheet to cover her more securely.

Sam stared at him in the dim light, her chest heaving as if from physical exertion, though he was the one who had been darting around the room. He reached toward her hair, and she captured his hand with her own, finally breaking her stillness as she wove her fingers with his.

He let out a ragged breath. "Sam…"

She didn't speak, but pulled him toward her, sitting up slightly as she drew his head closer. The sheet fell away until they were pressed against each other. His chest was cool against her burning skin, and she lifted her face to his.

Unlike their rushed kiss at the door, when Sam kissed Reed she drew him to her slowly, as if afraid he might bolt across the room at any moment. Her soft lips touched his, tentative after the previous hour, unsure of which steps to take and what lines to cross. As she continued stroking his lips with her own, the tension drained from his shoulders and he relaxed into her mouth. His arms encircled her, and his fingers pressed into her bare shoulders. He slipped into the small bed and lay behind her, still wearing his jeans.

His chest lay against the burning skin of her back, and Reed reached down to pull the sheet up, covering her as his arm draped over her naked body. His head lay next to hers on the pillow, and she felt him run his swollen lips along the nape of her neck as he nosed the hair away, inhaling deeply. His exhaustion creeped over her, and within a few minutes, they were fast asleep, lying next to each other in the fading moonlight.

CHAPTER SEVEN

Laguna Beach, California
March 2010

Kate used the key he had given her, opening the shop door later that night after hours of waiting to surprise him at his house. Moving silently through the front room, she hesitated, her heart fracturing a little more with each step and each familiar groan, as she approached the back room.

They were pressed against the back wall. The girl's legs were wrapped around his hips as she sat on the edge of the unfinished surfboard he had been working on. Beer bottles lay scattered, and a whiff of pot smoke lingered in the air.

They didn't see her for a few minutes, and her heart broke as Kate watched the man she thought she loved screw a nameless girl in the back of the shop his parents bought him.

She must have choked. Maybe she cried. But the girl's eyes lifted toward hers, and Cody's shoulders began to turn.

He only caught a glimpse of her wild hair as she disappeared into the night.

"Kate!"

Part Four:
The Sculptor

CHAPTER EIGHT

Pomona, California
May 2010

"Hello?" Kate had to shout over the pounding punk music that roared out of the warehouse. She pushed the door open, stepping into the dimly lit industrial studio.

"Mr. Lugo?"

The music seemed to be coming from one corner of the warehouse, so she walked carefully in that direction, dodging sheet metal, rebar and various concrete blocks scattered haphazardly around the huge space. She swallowed nervously as she approached the source of the noise, thinking perhaps Dee had been mistaken in directing her toward the notorious sculptor.

As she walked around a seemingly random corner created by cinder blocks and a reinforced steel door, she saw the sputtering light of a stick welder and the hulking form of the famous sculptor, Javier Lugo.

He was reaching upward, welding a massive piece that resembled a ragged flame turned upside down. The music continued to blare as he worked and a shower of sparks fell across his leather-shielded legs. His face was covered by a riotously painted helmet, and his arms were encased in the cow-hide sleeves typical of a working welder.

"Mr. Lugo?" she shouted again as the song changed.

The welder shut off immediately, the flickering blue star disappearing as he lifted his helmet and glared at her with angry black eyes.

"Who the hell are you?" he shouted. "Get out of my studio. This isn't a gallery."

"Ow!" Kate stubbed her toe on a partially broken cinder block as she continued walking toward him. "Um… my name is Kaitlyn Mitchell," she tried shouting over the song that had just started.

"What?" he yelled back. Setting his equipment down on a rolling cart next to him, he pulled off his thick leather gloves and picked up a remote control he used to turn the music off. The space echoed with quiet as he turned back toward her, scowling.

"Did Lydia send you? Are you from another fucking newspaper?" he asked, his deep voice echoing through the warehouse. Looking her up and down, from the toes of her canvas shoes to the Ray-Ban sunglasses that rested on her head, he grunted. "Shit, you're a student, aren't you?" He shook his head. "I don't use assistants, little girl. Go away."

He turned back toward the cart, picking up his gloves and flipping his helmet down.

"Wait! I'm Kate Mitchell, Dee's friend. She said she called you?" Kate's voice raised hopefully, though she was starting to doubt the cranky artist would tell her anything useful.

He paused, lifting his helmet again.

"Dee's friend?" His forehead furrowed in concentration. "I thought you were coming tomorrow. Wait, what day is it?"

"It's Saturday."

"Well, shit. No wonder Mari was pissed off," he muttered, throwing his gloves on the floor and pulling his brown sleeves off, revealing a sweat-drenched undershirt with no sleeves. He pulled his helmet off and set it on the cart. His hair was dark brown and closely cropped, and Kate watched him silently as he bent to remove the leather chaps that covered his jeans. He took a moment to stretch and rub his neck which had been kinked at an angle as he worked.

Javier Lugo was built like a bulldog, a massive one. His round head sat on a thick, muscular neck, and his broad shoulders were layered with the musculature he had developed from years of working with wood, metal, concrete, and stone. Though his hair and eyes were almost black, his skin was unexpectedly fair—and colorful, swirling tattoos marked his forearms and peeked from the back of his collar. He twisted his neck in either direction, and she heard it pop.

Kate winced at the painful sound, and he caught her out of the corner of his eye. A grim smirk crossed a face that would never be described as handsome. Kate saw the scar at the corner of his mouth turn up as he watched her. Javier Lugo may have been famous in art circles, but he would never be a celebrity.

"Not as pretty as O'Connor, am I?"

"Huh?" she asked, startled from her careful study of his square jawline. "What? Pretty? No, you're sort of… brutish-looking, aren't you?"

He let out a biting laugh and wiped his face with a red shop rag. She realized, as she walked closer to him, that though he wasn't much taller than her own five feet-four inches, his sheer physical presence and crackling energy dwarfed her. He walked over to a linoleum covered table with three mismatched chairs. Then he pulled out a Marlboro Red and lit it, finally sitting and gesturing to the chair across from him.

"You want a beer?"

Kate curled her lip. "It's ten o'clock in the morning."

"Well, I've been working here for the last two days straight, so I don't really give a flying fuck what time it is." He puffed out a stream of smoke. "Do you want a beer or not?"

Her mind flashed to a dark room filled with scattered beer bottles and smoke. She shoved the memory back and shrugged. "Sure, I guess."

"Great. Get me one, too. They're on the bottom shelf of the fridge over there." He nodded toward a corner of the warehouse where there was a sink, a work table with a steaming crock-pot, and a toaster oven. Next to the sink sat an old avocado-green refrigerator missing a handle.

Kate rolled her eyes, but walked over to the fridge, prying it open to find a treasure trove of beer. Imported. Artisan. She spotted a local brewery that her friends had raved about. There were also random bottles of hot sauce, but not much else. She grabbed two longnecks and walked back toward the table. The sculptor opened one bottle on the edge of the table and handed it to her before opening his own. She hid a smile at the surprisingly gallant gesture.

"Wait… you're twenty-one, right?" He squinted. "Hell, I don't actually care. Drink up. Here's to messed up pasts and old friends." He raised his bottle and took a long drink, gulping down half of the beer in one draw.

"I'm twenty-four. And thanks for the beer. You've got some good stuff in there."

"Yeah, well that's the best thing about selling shit, isn't it? I can afford to buy the good beer now. Never drink another Tecate, no matter what my uncle says about abandoning my heritage." He finished one cigarette and immediately lit another.

Her eyes roamed the cluttered warehouse, searching for something to break the awkward silence. They landed on the worn equipment he'd been using in his work.

"That's a nice welder. It's a Miller, right?" She nodded toward the blue welding unit he had been using.

He paused for a moment, his eyes lit in slight amusement. "Yeah, it is. I thought Dee said you were a photographer. Do you work with metal, too? How do you keep from falling over with all the gear on?"

Kate smiled. "That'd be a sight, huh? No, my dad—before he got really successful—he would take me out to job sites. He was a contractor. There was this one guy my dad worked with a really long time. He was a welder. He had this truck and he would fix any broken equipment, stuff like that."

The sculptor watched her in amusement, and a slightly indulgent look settled on his face.

"I remember Miller because that's the kind of welder he had. It was mounted on the side of the truck and I could read the name. I called him Mr. Miller for years. My dad eventually told me his name was Mr. West. I was kind of disappointed."

A wry smile twisted his lips as he shook his head.

"What does he do now?"

"Mr. Miller?"

He barked out a laugh. "No, your dad. You said, 'before he got successful.' What does he do now?"

"Oh, he's still a contractor. He just has a lot of different jobs now. He builds all over Orange County." She shrugged. "I don't think he ever goes to job sites anymore; he has foremen for that."

He studied her for a few moments, finishing his beer. "Well, good for him."

"I guess," she said, glancing back at the blue welder.

"There's nothing glamorous about breaking your back, you know."

"Is that why you're a sculptor instead of a mechanic?" she asked, remembering some of what Dee had told her about the thirty-six-year-old artist.

"Well, that and I like to buy the good beer." He stretched and stood up to grab another. The cigarette dangled from his mouth. "It's still not what my dad would consider a 'real job,' but it's better than being a surf bum or an actor, you know?"

She snorted. "Tell me about it."

He cocked an eyebrow at her, as if surprised by the bitterness of her tone. "I thought all you Orange County girls liked the surfers." He smirked as he sat back down at the table. "Or was it an actor who made that pretty little mouth frown?"

"No one." Kate gave him a hard look. "It was no one."

They sat in silence for a few minutes, their eyes measuring the other across the scarred table. Kate could tell that Javier Lugo knew she wanted something from him, but she had no interest in flattery and had the feeling the man wouldn't be impressed with it anyway. He didn't seem to care what she thought of him. Kate realized that she didn't really care what he thought of her, either. And really, not caring about his opinion felt like a refreshing change.

Javier leaned back, stretching his stocky legs in front of him as he took another drink. "When I was in school, we were all so incestuous. We always dated other artists. Usually visual artists. Musicians were okay. Dancers *weren't*. Strictly speaking, photographers were a little looked down on." He grinned and winked at her shocked expression.

She shifted in her seat and rolled her eyes a little. "Well, moving past odd dating trivia, Mr. Lugo—"

"Oh fuck!" He snorted beer through his nose as Kate dodged the spray, visibly disgusted. "It's just Javi, all right? Everyone calls me Javi. Even stick-in-the-mud Bradley doesn't call me Mr. Lugo. My sister would laugh her ass off."

"Professor Bradley's not a 'stick-in-the-mud.'" Kate defended her advisor.

Javi looked at her sympathetically. "Yes, he is. Of *course* he is. But he's a nice stick-in-the-mud, and that counts for something." He paused to light another cigarette. "Most importantly, he adores Dee, so that gives him points in my book. Thank God the baby looks like her, though."

Kate snickered, but quickly tried to rein back the artist's wandering narrative. "Did Dee tell you why I wanted to talk to you?"

"Yeah," Javi said as he exhaled a long stream of smoke. "Sort of. Seriously, though, I don't know if anything I tell you is going to help with your thesis. If Dee didn't ask me, I wouldn't give you the time of day."

"Why doesn't that surprise me?"

"What?" He coughed and scratched at the back of his neck. "You think your idol would? Reed's a bigger asshole than me. And a hermit. He's just a good-looking one, so people let him get away with it. They call him 'mercurial' and 'enigmatic' instead of 'pissy' and 'rude.'"

"You don't sound like you like him very much."

"Of course I like him. He's one of my best friends." He took another draw on his Marlboro. "Doesn't mean I think he's particularly nice, though."

Kate raised her eyebrows in amusement. "So, does Reed O'Connor have any good qualities?"

Javi looked her in the eye. "He's brilliant, and he's not cocky about it. He's generous—way more than he would ever let on." He paused to take another swallow of beer. "To the people that matter to him, Reed O'Connor one of the most loyal people you will ever meet. Ever. That's what made the whole thing so nuts."

"What thing?" Kate asked quickly.

Javi waved a dismissive hand. "Dee says you remind her of Reed. I've never seen you work, so I can't say one way or another, but since she practically walks on water, in my not-humble-at-all opinion, I'll take her word for it."

Kate sighed in disappointment before she shrugged. "I admire O'Connor's work. I think it says a lot about the twisted concepts of beauty in our society."

"Really?"

"Yeah, really." She met his gaze unflinchingly.

"So, little girl—"

"I'm not a little girl. My name is Kate."

His mouth twisted in a smile. "So, Katie… if you were O'Connor—which you're not, but let's pretend—what part of my face would you photograph? Remember"—he lifted his chin in challenge—"never the whole face. That gives too much away."

"One frame?"

"One frame to capture who you think I am."

Kate cocked her head at him, studying him for a few moments as they sat in tense silence. She reached over to pull his chin down a little and tilt his head forward. His chin was covered in a course stubble, and his black eyes studied her face as she concentrated.

"Here," she said softly, making her fingers into a rectangle and leaning back. "Your jaw from the side angle, encompassing your neck and the top of your collarbone."

"And why is that your frame?" he murmured.

"Your jaw is the most prominent feature of your face, except your eyes" She glanced up to meet them. "Which are too revealing. Your neck is thickly muscled, indicating the physical nature of your work, and there's a slight scattering of tiny scars along your collarbone from where I imagine you started welding on something without your helmet. You had an idea. You couldn't wait to put on your safety equipment. Maybe you were just wearing glasses, or holding the helmet to the flame."

Her eyes lifted, and their gazes locked for a moment. Kate was stunned by the spark that jumped between them.

"I mean… that's what might have happened," she whispered.

Javi broke away first and leaned back, reaching for another cigarette. After he lit it, he inhaled deeply before blowing out a line of smoke. "What's your question?" he asked quietly.

Kate sat up straight. "I only get one?"

"Maybe. It depends on what question you ask."

"Fine. Who was Samantha Rhodes to Reed O'Connor?"

A slow smile grew on his face. "Now *that* is a very good question."

"So, what's the answer?"

"Which one do you want?"

"If it's a good question, I want the good answer."

Javi chuckled. "You do remind me of him, a little. I see what Dee was talking about." He exhaled another stream of smoke. "What was Sam to Reed? Hmm. The short answer would be his girlfriend, but the *good* answer would be, what wasn't she?"

"What do you mean?"

Javi's eyes started to drift around the studio. "Before he met her, Reed was brilliant, just… fucking brilliant." He frowned, shaking his head a little. "We met at an art show in L.A. before he started at Foothill. He's a couple years younger than me, but I liked him. He wasn't part of the 'in-crowd,' so to speak. He could've done anything, really. He downplayed all his other talents because he liked photography so much, but he was good at almost everything. He could draw; he could sculpt. Not as good as me, but he was pretty damn good. Surprisingly good at ceramics, of all things. And that was before he met Sam."

"And after?"

He took another draw on his cigarette. "After? Shit, that's when he found his genius. That perfect vision married with his technical skills and focused by this incredible passion. What was Sam to Reed?" Javi shrugged, shaking his head back and forth. "His muse, his passion... Probably the love of his life—not that we had any idea what that meant when we were that age."

"What do you mean?"

His eyes narrowed as he looked at her. "We were so young; we just took it for granted. How the hell were we supposed to know we would never feel anything like that again?"

"I don't—feel what?" Kate frowned. "What are you talking about?"

"That crazy energy they had." He leaned forward. "Both of them were brilliant separately, but then put them together? They were like a—a battery or a reactor or something. They charged us all. Our whole damn group: me, Vanessa, Dee, Suz, even Bradley's work got better. And their own stuff? Pure genius. I can't—"

He broke off, leaning back in his chair as he collected himself, shaking his head with regret. "There's no way to describe it, Katie. It's impossible."

Kate sat back in her chair, consumed with regret for a loss she could feel down to her bones. She had to clear her throat before she spoke. "What the hell happened to them?"

A flicker of pain crossed his face. He took another drink of his beer. "Human," he said hoarsely, glancing up into her eyes again before staring at his feet. "They were just... human."

Kate stared at him, but he didn't look back. Finally, she stood and walked to the fridge, helping herself to another beer and wiping the unexpected tears from her eyes. She grabbed one for Javi as well and walked back, sitting down as he opened them on the edge of the scarred table.

"So, what's this you're working on?" she asked, gesturing to the inverted flame which seemed to burn in the background.

He watched her for a moment before he smiled. "Beer money."

Kate and Javi launched into a hesitant discussion of his work, but eventually they relaxed. After a couple of hours sharing jokes and stories about Chris and Dee in college, he even offered to show her his personal gallery.

"Every artist has one, you know," he said over his shoulder as he led her toward the back of the warehouse. "Whether they do it deliberately or not. We all have pieces that are too personal to sell or even give away."

"Thanks." She smiled at him. "For showing me your stuff, I mean. I really appreciate it."

He shrugged, turning on the light in what was once a small office. Scattered around the room were small sculptures in marble, wood and a few metal pieces. In one corner was a case of delicate gold and silver jewelry. Kate slowly walked around the room until one sculpture caught her attention.

"Wow, that's—is that based on Dee's photograph of them?" She pointed to the wooden sculpture done in a fine grained, golden wood. The curved figures were abstract and the faces indistinct, but the figures' position was exactly that of the revealing picture of Reed and Sam she had seen in Dee's studio.

Javi looked at her in surprise. "Oh, you've seen that? Um... yeah. I have to put this one away on the rare occasions Reed comes back to town. I did that one years ago. He had that picture hanging up in his apartment for a while, and I remembered seeing it."

He stood in front of the sculpture, leaning his head to mimic the slant of the piece. "I loved the angles in it. Two perfectly melded into one, you know? And the way their arms were... This is an old one. I was doing a lot of wood carving back then."

She gazed again at the figures as she walked around the piece, imagining she could see the two lovers in the three dimensions not captured in the photograph.

"It's stunning," she said wistfully.

Javi cleared his throat. "I should probably..." He shook his head and turned to the jewelry case, waving her over. "Come here."

Kate smiled. "You do silver and gold-smithing, too? That's amazing."

"Why?"

"Be—because of... Well, the sculpture stuff is so big and this —" She waved her hand at the intricate jewelry. "It's just so small and delicate. How do you do it?"

Javi looked at her for a moment before he shrugged. "Most sculptors study metal-smithing. It's just another form of sculpture. Did… did Dee mention you were going to see Vanessa this week?" Javi looked at her sideways, rubbing the tattoos on the back of his neck.

"Yeah, I am. I'm meeting her at her studio in Hollywood tomorrow."

He cleared his throat. "Could you deliver a piece to her for me? I did some work for her a while back and never got a chance to give it to her. I'd appreciate it if you could." He smiled a little. "Pay me back for the beer, you know."

Kate shrugged. "Sure. No problem."

He nodded and opened a drawer in the bottom of the case, taking a small, cloth-wrapped package from it and quickly handing it to Kate. She took the piece and put it in her pocket before they returned to the kitchen.

Kate gathered her things to go, and Javi walked her out through his maze of a studio.

"You could get lost for days in this junk pile, little girl."

"I actually think it's kind of cool." Kate looked around. It was cluttered, but not dirty. The whole building was a riot of texture and angle, a mess of parts that added up to a surprisingly intriguing setting. Then her eyes fell on Javi, who was watching her with an inexplicable frown.

"You think this place is cool?"

She suddenly felt shy, so she kept walking. "Yeah, kinda."

When they reached the door to the outside, he put his hand out and she shook it.

"Javi, thanks for… just thanks. I appreciate you talking to me."

"No problem." He shrugged. "Well, yeah, it was sort of irritating, but not as bad as I thought."

Kate just smiled and walked to her car, glancing at him as he stood in the dim shadow created by the door of the warehouse. She realized she must have driven by his studio a thousand times and never looked at it, never realized that an artist of his stature lived so close by.

She stared at him. "I guess…"

He leaned forward as if he was about to step into the sunlight. "Yeah?"

Her eyes met his and she felt a sudden pull, but she carefully took another step toward her car. "I'll see you around."

His mouth twisted into a smile. "Yeah. I'll see you."

CHAPTER NINE

Claremont, California
May 2000

"Please, Dee? Please, please, please? I'll make you whatever jewelry you want," Javi whined and wheedled, trying to persuade his friend to take the pictures he so desperately needed for his portfolio the next week.

Dee huffed impatiently and went back to cooking the chicken biryani everyone had clamored for earlier. "What kind of jewelry?" she asked, glancing at Chris who sat at the table with Susan and Vanessa, waiting for dinner. Chris winked at her, eliciting a small, rueful smile.

The sculptor continued, "Remember that turquoise I got? I'll make something out of that for you. A necklace. Or a bracelet if you want. Just please take the pictures. I don't trust anyone else."

She sighed. "Really, Javi, I'm not joking about this! I'm *so* swamped this weekend. Why don't you ask Reed?"

Javi snorted in disgust. "Reed?"

The man in question walked into the open apartment, stopping in the kitchen to snag a piece of chicken out of the pan. "What about me?" he asked as Dee slapped at his hand.

Javi curled his lip. "I was just about to tell Dee how you don't have time to do anything for your friends anymore."

"What? I'm just on a productive streak right now. Don't mess with it, asshole." Reed kissed Dee on top of her head and walked back toward Sam's room. He knocked on the closed door. "You ready?"

Sam answered the door in a loose outfit of shorts and a t-shirt. She was wearing flip-flops and her hair fell loose over her shoulders. "Yeah," she said. "Let's go."

The two waved at the group sitting at the table and walked out the door and down the stairs.

Susan piped up. "Who else saw that one coming?"

"She had the 'friends' talk with me over two weeks ago. I bet that's when it started," Chris said from the corner of the kitchen table, eyeing Dee as she plated the food.

"You all assume…" Vanessa murmured. "Sam's sat for me dozens of times; she's beautiful and a great model."

"'Sitting for him,' huh?" Javi walked past Vanessa, stooping down to give the statuesque brunette a flirtatious kiss on the cheek. "Is that what they're calling it nowadays?"

The five friends dug into dinner as Reed and Sam walked silently to his small apartment. Their hands brushed each other's as they walked, and they cast lingering glances in the late afternoon sun.

As they entered the room, Reed shut the door and swung around to pull Sam against his chest, kissing and lifting her as she wrapped her legs around his waist. He moved them to the small bed and leaned over her, ridding her body of the loose-fitting garments as his full lips traced her curves, tasting each hidden corner while her hands worked to unbutton his jeans.

Sam pulled at his shirt, almost ripping it in her desperate hurry to feel his skin against her own. He pushed her farther onto the bed before he drew back, staring as the setting sun spilled over her breasts. She caught his look of concentration and lay still as he reached for the camera that lay beside the bed. He quickly captured the image of her skin, stained by the afternoon light, then he leaned down and placed the camera on the floor before he returned his attention to Sam. His mouth slicked over her warm skin until she moaned in impatience, finally shoving his pants down and pulling him closer.

They moved together, a sinuous tangle of limbs, crying each other's names into the afternoon air, consumed with each other as they made love and the sun painted the walls gold.

CHAPTER TEN

Claremont, California
May 2010

"Kaitlyn, for the last time, will you answer the boy's calls? This has got to be some sort of misunderstanding. Barbara and I are both just sick about you two breaking up. I know what a good boy Cody—"

Kate pressed delete on her phone before her mother started reciting her ex-boyfriend's many virtues... again. She should probably call and finally tell them why she broke up with Cody. After all, it had been two months.

She'd gone over and over why he had cheated on her. Once upon a time, they'd been in love. At least, that's what it had seemed like to her. He'd been encouraging. Enthusiastic about her work, even if he'd never really understood it. Cody was a good guy. The kind who called his mom and helped old ladies load their groceries into their cart. He'd helped Kate, too.

What had changed?

Had it been that fact that he'd wanted to move forward and she hadn't? What had been holding her back? Maybe there was something wrong with *her*. After all, Cody was a *really* nice guy.

"Before he was a cheating douchebag," she muttered.

She sat in the small breakfast nook of her apartment, ridiculously glad she had never agreed to leave it and move in with him, as she continued to listen to her messages.

"Kate, babe—"

Delete.

"Katie girl, it's Dad." She smiled at her father's welcome voice. *"I have a feeling I know what might have happened considering I saw a snot-nosed kid that used to be lucky enough to date my daughter having lunch with some bimbo in Laguna yesterday."* He paused, and Kate held back the tears threatening to leak down her face. *"I'm sorry, kiddo. For what it's worth, I think he was too boring for you, and I know you were always too smart for him. He probably knew that better than anyone."* Her dad cleared his throat on the recording. *"Also, I always thought he used too much shit in his hair. Call me when you want to talk, bye."*

She snorted at her dad's mention of Cody's elaborate hair rituals. She thought about it, deciding it *was* annoying that her ex-boyfriend spent more time getting ready in the morning than she did. She noticed one more message from an unknown number in her voicemail. She touched it and listened, waiting over a long pause at the beginning of the message. She thought for sure it would be a junk call and was about to delete it when she heard his voice.

"Uh, yeah, Kaitlyn. I mean, Katie—Kate. I got your number from Dee. So... you left some shit at my place. I don't know if you need it or not." There was another long pause in the message. *"So, yeah. Call me if you want. My number's 555-4537. You can come get your stuff. 'Cause it's here."* Long pause. *"Bye."* Another pause. *"This is Javi Lugo."* Click.

Kate frowned. Well, that was... interesting.

Part Five:
The Painter

CHAPTER ELEVEN

Los Angeles, California
May 2010

Kate sat at a small table outside the restaurant in Hollywood, taking shelter from the already sweltering sun under the covered patio. She sipped her iced tea and glanced at the clock on her phone. She was a little early to meet Vanessa Allensworth, but she was passing by the small restaurant when the painter called asking if they could meet for lunch, so Kate had suggested meeting her there.

Within a few minutes, Kate's eyes caught the tall figure of the artist as she made her way down the street. If you didn't know who she was, Vanessa Allensworth could have been easily mistaken for a model, though her statuesque figure would never be considered fashionable on a modern runway. Her light brown skin glowed in the California sun. She was a stunning woman, easily five feet-ten inches, her dark curls framed dramatic features that begged to be photographed, and her steps were long and sure.

As she drew nearer, Kate noted that, far from the smudged work clothes that most of her friends wore while painting, Ms. Allansworth wore a flowing red dress that epitomized bohemian chic. A kind smile lit her face when she spotted Kate, and she waved.

"You must be Kate," she said as she approached the table. "Dee said to look for your gorgeous hair. You look like a pre-Raphaelite model, you're so fair. Have you ever modeled?"

"No, I don't think the pre-Raphaelites specialized in freckles, did they?" Kate joked, surprised by the compliment. The tall painter immediately set her at ease with her grace and quiet confidence. She sat down at the small patio table, and Kate watched her carefully arrange the drape of her dress. "Honestly, that's really flattering, but I prefer to be behind the lens."

Vanessa's mouth quirked up into a smile. "Well, that reminds me of someone else I know. Thank you for meeting me here, by the way. I've been working all morning, and I lost track of time. I'm starving."

The waitress came over to get Vanessa's drink order. The painter ordered a glass of white wine and asked for a few more minutes to look over the menu. Kate took a minute to study the woman across from her.

Vanessa Allensworth had achieved national recognition almost immediately upon graduating by virtue of her very famous parents. Her modern depictions of the feminine form were praised by critics and prized across the country. Her shows were attended by the elite of the art world. She was an Angelino by birth and had chosen to remain in L.A. to work. She came from a family of prominent artists. Her mother was a poet; her father directed films. Kate also knew from talking with Dee that, of all the people who had known Sam Rhodes in school, Vanessa was one of the few she kept in regular contact with.

"Do you know what you're having?" Vanessa asked.

"Just a salad, I think. I can never eat much when it's hot."

"If only that worked for me. I'd have a much better figure during bathing suit season."

"Are you kidding? You're beautiful. You shouldn't change anything."

"Thank you. I'm being self-deprecating. I'm not really that modest. It is interesting, though. Photographers usually think I'm more beautiful than other people. I've always wondered why."

"We like dramatic features. Did Reed O'Connor ever photograph you?"

The waitress walked up to take their orders, and Kate waited patiently. Vanessa, she noticed, was very specific as she ordered her egg white omelet. It fit with the meticulous impression the painter projected.

"Yes," Vanessa finally answered after the waitress left. "Reed has photographed me a number of times over the years. He did one I love for my first major show in New York. Though I hated it when I first saw it." She smiled. "That's quite common, you know. Many of his subjects don't like his portraits at first."

"What is it? The one you liked—what was the picture?"

Vanessa turned her head to the side and looked at Kate out of the corner of her eye. "It was a profile, but only of my nose and forehead. The rest of my face was shadowed. I was absolutely furious with him at first. He knew I'd never liked my nose."

"Really?" Kate frowned. "I was just thinking at that particular angle I could almost see a crown on your head. Your profile is very—"

"Regal?" Vanessa interrupted with a smile, and Kate nodded. "Yes, that exactly what he said, too. 'Vanessa,' he said in that infuriatingly calm voice of his, 'don't you see you're a queen when I photograph you?'" She smiled at the memory. "That was maybe three years after Reed and Sam moved to New York. He was still developing his style, doing commercial fashion work, but all the right people were already taking notice. He was extraordinary. And his focus tended to be…" she paused. "*Softer* than it is now, I think. Still his style. Always his style. His photographs have always been distinctive."

"It's one of the reasons his work fascinates me. You can't mistake his eye for anyone else." Kate leaned her elbow on the table, studying the woman across from her. Suddenly, she sat up. "Oh, before I forget…" She reached into her messenger bag. "I have a delivery for you. From Javi Lugo. I talked to him yesterday."

"Javi, huh? You're catching all the old gang, aren't you?" Her hand extended as Kate held out the small, cloth-wrapped package. Vanessa took it and placed it on her lap, peeking at it quickly.

Kate had quashed her natural curiosity, refusing to open the small package while it was in her care. She was unable to see what was in the mysterious delivery, though she observed the enigmatic smile that crossed Vanessa's face before she wrapped it again to place in her purse.

After a few moments, Vanessa spoke again. "Dee said you were doing some research into Reed's background for your project. I have to tell you, I don't feel comfortable telling you anything that's going to be published. He's quite a private person, and I consider him a friend, so—"

"I'm not going to publish anything about his background." Kate was quick to reassure her. "It's more for my own understanding. The content of my thesis hasn't changed significantly, I just…" Kate trailed off, at a loss to explain her exact reasons for searching out the origins of the mysterious portrait. "Professor Bradley said something a few weeks ago, and I noticed some things about a few of his pictures. I feel like I don't have as clear an understanding of his work as I once did, I guess."

Vanessa gave her a measuring look. "What did Chris say to you?"

"He said that to understand Reed O'Connor, I had to understand Samantha Rhodes." She waited for the other woman to respond. Vanessa took a sip of her wine and set it down thoughtfully. "Was he right?"

Vanessa stared at her for a few moments. "Chris always was a wise old man. A good observer. And a better photographer than anyone ever gave him credit for, I think. I expect he's a very good teacher, isn't he?"

"He is. Miss Allansworth—"

"You may call me Vanessa, Kate." She paused, still looking at the young woman with consideration. "I'll give you my observations of them both, as much as I'm comfortable with, but let's wait and talk more back at my studio. It's more private."

Kate nodded. "Of course."

Their waitress came back with their food and Vanessa smiled at her politely. "Perfect timing. Thank you."

The two women spent the next hour talking about their work. As fascinated as Kate was by Vanessa's brilliance and experience, Vanessa seemed to be equally enthralled by Kate's perspective and excitement. In no time, the meal had passed and they began to walk back to Vanessa's studio in North Hollywood. As they walked, Kate contemplated the seeming serendipity of so many unusually talented artists coming out of the same small art school in the foothills of Southern California. According to Dee, most of them had even lived in the same building.

"Vanessa, doesn't it seem strange that you and Javier Lugo, and Reed O'Connor and Sam Rhodes all graduated at the same time? You're all nationally known now—not Rhodes as much, she's more regionally known—but everyone else…"

"Yes," Vanessa said. "It's unusual, I suppose. Javi"…" She chuckled. "Javi would give most of the credit to Reed and Sam, and all that amazing energy they had."

"Is he right?" Kate asked as the painter pulled the door open to her air-conditioned building. They walked inside, and Vanessa went to put her purse in the small kitchen near the front of the studio.

She paused for a moment as she walked back toward Kate. "Partly. He's *partly* right. Reed and Sam did create this kind of magnetic hum around them, and they attracted very talented people as friends, but giving them too much credit doesn't give the rest of us enough, I think. We're all *very* talented. I'm not being pompous; we just are. And you have to give credit to Lydia, don't ever forget Lydia," Vanessa cautioned with a shake of her head.

"Lydia Collins, right? She represents all of you?"

"Yes," Vanessa nodded. "She's knew us all in college—well, she and I knew each other growing up—and she's an extraordinary businesswoman. Her family has been in the business for ages."

"Maybe I'll meet her someday."

"It would be to your benefit if she likes you." Vanessa continued. "Lydia knows almost everyone in the art world. She's very well connected, and she works very hard for her artists."

"So it wasn't all about the Reed and Sam magic?" Kate asked, smiling as they continued into Vanessa's work area. There were a number of canvases in all stages of completion, exhibiting the rich colors and bold strokes the artist was known for. Kate moved around the room, taking in the strictly organized space where the painter worked. Though the pervasive smell of turpentine tinged the air, it was, without a doubt, the cleanest studio Kate had ever seen.

"Do you want a bottle of water?" Vanessa asked from across the room.

"No, thank you." Kate leaned in, examining a strangely familiar abstract that glowed with rich red, gold and purple oils. She squinted at the angles and cocked her head as she examined it. "Hey, Vanessa, is this—"

"Reed and Sam?" she asked from right over Kate's shoulder. The younger woman jumped a little and turned around to see Vanessa smiling at her and drinking a small green bottle of Perrier.

"Yes. Is it?"

She nodded. "It's my interpretation of that wonderful sculpture Javi did, which was based on that picture Dee took of them when we were in school." She grinned. "We're all thieves, you know. Constantly ripping ideas off from each other. Feeding on each other like parasites." She laughed, and Kate smiled at her amusement.

Vanessa went to sit down at a small bistro table in the corner of the room. The arched window behind her was lined with clear glass jars holding various-sized paint brushes. The afternoon sun shone through and cast intriguing shadows on the terra-cotta floor.

Kate sat in the other chair. "Did you feel it? The energy that Javi and Dee talked about. Did it affect your work, too?"

"Yes, though not always in a good way. I learned quite early that I didn't work as well if I had too much going on around me. Everyone's different. Some people like to have music playing, or the television going in the background. Some people like working with people around them, and others like utter isolation." She smiled at Kate. "I'm more of an utter isolation person."

Kate nodded and waited for her to continue.

"I found the energy they put out to be almost too much, most of the time. No, they inspired me, but it wasn't because of that."

Kate paused to make sure the painter had finished speaking. "What was it, then?"

Vanessa smiled wistfully, looking across the studio at the painting hanging on the wall. "They just *loved* each other so deeply, Kate. That's what inspired me, not the manic energy, which was probably a reflection of their amazing sexual chemistry. That was a big part of their relationship, don't get me wrong, but it wasn't their *whole* relationship."

Kate concentrated on Vanessa as she reminisced.

"If you didn't know them, it might be all you saw—the sexual energy. But they had an extraordinarily deep love, as well. They took care of each other. They were very protective of their relationship, especially around new people."

Kate fought back the unexpected sting of grief. "What do you think happened to them? Do you know why they separated?"

The sorrow was evident when Vanessa spoke again. "It's hard to say. Something shifted with them, after they went to New York. I'm not sure what, and it wasn't because one of them wanted to go and one didn't. They were both excited to move after graduation. No, something happened. Something that dimmed what they had."

"And you have no idea?"

Vanessa shrugged. "I've heard bits and pieces of what caused the actual breakup, but I wasn't there, so I don't know for sure. I think the only witness was that assistant Reed used for a short time, Brandon Wylie." The painter sighed. "Really, Kate, only two people ever know what goes on in a relationship. The rest of us can only speculate. And I'm not really a fan of speculation."

Kate sat, studying the shadows on the floor, lost in her own thoughts.

"I do know that they loved each other, though. Even when there were things going on at the end. They really, *really* loved each other. In fact, knowing both of them now, I don't think they've ever stopped loving each other."

"Even now?" Kate asked. She felt a strange flutter of hope in her chest.

Vanessa smiled. "Don't quote me on that. After all, I'm not a fan of speculation."

CHAPTER TWELVE

Claremont, California
August 2000

Reed lay naked, propped in a corner of the bed while, across from him, Sam sat in a rickety chair wearing one of his t-shirts. She was sketching him. Again. His leg was bent and he relaxed, his arms folded behind his head as he stared at his girlfriend of four months.

"Why did you put clothes on? If I have to lie here completely still, you should at least let me look at you naked."

"If I was naked, you'd be more tempted to grab your camera, which would defeat the whole 'lying still' thing," Sam muttered. "You have very long legs, Reed."

"I do. But then, I seem to remember you praising my proportions earlier this afternoon."

She shook her head, but he caught her eyes examining him. He smiled when they traced over his face, across his chest, and down his abdomen before they explored further south. He watched her from across the room and wondered just how long she could keep him in bed sketching before she gave into temptation.

"You could have sex all day, couldn't you, Reed?"

"No, I could take pictures of you naked… and have sex all day."

"Well, it's good to know you have diverse interests."

He smiled at her. He loved the way her hair lay in gold waves over her shoulders. She had perfect shoulders, he thought, and her hair never quite curled, but always seemed to tease that it might. Her strong features were furrowed in concentration as she worked, and he thought again how lucky he was to have found someone who suited him so unexpectedly.

He loved her. He'd realized it the other day, but was still unsure when or how he should tell her. She was the first person he had ever been in love with, and it was much more overwhelming than he had expected. How should he tell her? Reed didn't know whether he was supposed to make an occasion out of it. Should he take her out for dinner? Get down on one knee? He was pretty sure that was only for proposing. He thought he should probably just tell her. Not during sex, though. He had a feeling he wasn't supposed to do that.

The tip of Sam's tongue peeked out of the corner of her mouth as she concentrated. He was surprised by how much her attention didn't bother him. For most of his childhood, Reed had been different, and he normally hated being the center of anyone's attention. With Sam, though, he didn't mind. It was probably because of the love thing.

"Sam?" he whispered, deliberately trying to break her concentration. "Samantha."

"Reed," she whispered back. "Be quiet. Stop trying to distract me. I'm almost done."

"Well, I'm almost ready to go again. Good timing." He reached down to indicate a new focus for her attention and smirked when he saw her glance. Sam rolled her eyes again, but Reed caught her hungry look.

She finished her sketch with a small frown between her eyebrows. Then she took a deep breath and closed her book, smiling at him as she finished. "Thanks, baby."

He crooked his finger at her. "Come here."

She set her book down, along with her pencils. "Over there?" she asked innocently.

He nodded, continuing to curl a long finger at her, then he grinned and added another, curling two fingers in a suggestive motion. She laughed, but began to walk toward him. Reed mouthed, 'Come, come, come,' his full lips curling around the words and his blue eyes narrowing playfully. Giving in to temptation, she crawled on the bed and crept toward him on all fours.

As soon as she was in range of his arms, Reed grabbed her. Sam squealed in delight as he rolled her under his naked body on the rumpled bed. He took his time to explore every inch of her face with his mouth as she laughed and wiggled under him. He paused before he got to her lips and looked into her eyes. His expression softened as he stared at her.

"What?" She giggled quietly.

"Do you know what my favorite part of your face is?"

"No, you've photographed my mouth, my eyes, my jaw. I have no idea at this point," she said, still laughing.

"All of it together. That's my favorite part. I like your eyes." He bent down and kissed her eyelids tenderly. "I like your nose." He laughed as she wrinkled it, but he kissed that, too. "I *really* like your mouth." She stuck her tongue out at him, but he captured it between his teeth, turning it into a deep kiss until she was moaning and arching under him. When he finally drew away, they were both panting and smiling.

He moved his mouth down along her jaw and neck. "Your neck is beautiful. The skin is so soft," he murmured. "Your ears." Reed's lips moved over and he nibbled the lobe gently. "Your ears are so damn cute. But it all goes together to make one..." He kissed her mouth again and reached up to frame her face with his hands. "Perfectly beautiful face."

"Reed," she whispered breathlessly and pulled him down to kiss her again. His lips began moving lower. His hands stroked along her skin as he deftly removed the shirt she had thrown on earlier. He could feel her arching against his body, searching for friction when his mouth reached her breasts.

"More," she cried, pulling his face up toward hers and moving their bodies into perfect alignment. Sam cried out when he entered her. She wrapped her legs around his hips so they moved in rhythm, and his whispered words covered her as thoroughly as his body.

"Sammy..." She opened her eyes to meet his own. Reed felt as if his heart would explode as he watched her eyes darken in pleasure. She gasped, and he felt her body clench around him in as he moved in her; it tipped him over the edge and he groaned into her mouth when he came. As his breath evened out, Reed rolled them on their sides so he could gather her close to his chest. Then after his heart had calmed, he turned her around, and his lips continued to pepper her shoulder with kisses until he felt her relax.

Sam sighed in contentment as she fell asleep. Reed whispered against her skin and followed her soon after.

The next morning, he woke when he felt her crawl over him. The morning light poured through the open window as she sat on the edge of the bed.

"Hey, good morning. Where are you going?" he asked, his voice hoarse with sleep. He cleared his throat, watching how the light touched her shoulder and automatically reaching down for the camera that lay on the floor by his bed. He grabbed it and began taking pictures of her as she rubbed the sleep from her eyes. The light caught the small tendrils of hair that curled behind her ear, making them glow, and her skin was luminous in the morning light.

"I promised Vanessa I'd sit for her today. She's got a watercolor assignment she says would suit my coloring, so I said I'd help. She wanted to do it first thing this morning."

He hummed absently as he continued clicking pictures with one hand. His other hand ran up and down her back, making her shiver.

"Reed..." She arched, her body automatically responding to his touch. "I have to go, baby."

"Not yet," he whispered. "Sammy..." His hand reached up to grasp her shoulder and she tilted her head toward him, a smile starting to grow on her face. His camera continued to click automatically as he continued, "Sammy, I love you."

She turned, smiling with quiet joy. Grabbing his camera, she placed it beside him on the bed and stroked his face with her hand, scratching lightly at his dark stubble. She leaned toward him, capturing his lips with her own.

"I love you, too."

CHAPTER THIRTEEN

Pomona, California
May 2010

"I can't believe you've never been to the art walk before."

Kate met Javi on Saturday night in front of the old Fox Theater on Third Street. He had given her the small bag of lens caps and filters that had fallen out of her backpack before persuading her to walk around for a bit. She found that she didn't need much convincing as she looked around at the lively street fair.

"I just don't come down in this direction much. I'm either at school or in Orange County." Though, upon further reflection, she realized breaking up with Cody was going to free up a lot of her time.

The more she thought about their relationship, the more Kate realized most of it had revolved around Cody. He hardly ever came to her place in Claremont, and it was easy to make the forty minute drive to his house when most of her family lived close by anyway. In fact, most of her family and all her old friends still lived within a few miles of each other.

As she strolled through the Pomona Arts Colony, she realized she had spent more time driving in the past five years than she had appreciating the rich cultural mix that made up Southern California's Inland Valley.

She caught the smell of sesame oil mixing with the rich spices of traditional Mexican food. A barbecue stand on the corner was occupied by a tall, black man with a Southern accent, who was laughing with a young man wearing a fedora and a guitar strapped to his back. A myriad of languages swirled around her as she wandered through the old downtown, which had been transformed over the previous fifteen years by the unlikely gathering of artists and musicians.

"You're almost out of college. Time to start hanging out with some real artists." Javi nodded toward a young man who had some sort of plywood wall set up on the street. He was using spray-paint to layer graffiti and, as Kate watched, the young artist handed the paint can to a woman old enough to be his grandmother and gestured to the wall. The old woman laughed, but tentatively took the can and sprayed a little red paint on the makeshift piece of art as the young man grinned.

Kate was smiling when she looked back at Javi, who was watching her with a curious expression on his face.

"What?"

He started walking again. Frowning at the taciturn sculptor, she hurried to catch up with him. "Why do you live in Pomona?"

"Why do you want to know?"

She shrugged. "I guess I'm just curious."

He gave a wave to a woman selling tamales on the corner. "You're curious about a lot, aren't you?"

"Yes."

He turned to her with a smirk. "Do you have a thing for O'Connor?"

Her mouth fell open. "What? No! Why—I mean, why do you think that?"

"You ask a lot of questions about him, that's all." He shrugged. "That asshole always had tail chasing him in school."

"No, I've never had a 'thing' for him. Besides, he's kind of larger-than-life, you know? It's not like I'll ever meet him."

Javi laughed outright. "Why on earth do you say that? You hang out with the closest thing that guy has to friends."

Kate was speechless for a moment as she considered his words. Finally, she turned to him. "I—I don't want to talk about O'Connor, okay?"

Javi stared back for a moment before he turned to keep walking down Thomas Street. She joined him, silently taking in the chaotic atmosphere of the Art Walk. The sounds of music met them at the corner, but they kept walking past the group that had gathered around the three street performers.

"Why do I live here?" he finally said. "I guess because… there's still more mechanics than hipsters."

"What?" she asked with a laugh.

"You heard me. There's the Arts Colony, yeah. And don't get me wrong, I like being around artists as much as I like being around anyone—"

"Which is not all that much, I'm guessing."

He shrugged. "Most people are annoying."

"Am I supposed to be flattered?"

He looked at her out of the corner of his eye. "Why would you be flattered? I never said I liked you."

She snorted. "Cranky old man."

"Annoying little girl."

She rolled her eyes at him and saw the corner of his mouth turn up. "So, you live in Pomona…"

Pausing to let a group of teenagers skate past, he finally answered. "I guess it reminds me of where I grew up in L.A. but not as much of the bad stuff, you know?"

"What—"

"Never mind, you don't know. Gangs, little girl. Lots of gangs and drugs and shit like that." Javi nodded at a group of young painters who were huddled together at a booth. Two of them were sketching, and one was talking to a woman about a painting in vivid greens and blues. The painter waved at them enthusiastically.

Kate glanced at the contradictory sculptor by her side. "Okay."

"There's still a lot of that here, but something more, I guess. People here want to be better."

They kept walking past the artists and the vendors, dodging kids and a few dogs as they made their way down the street. Every now and then, someone would call Javi's name or point at him, but he mostly ignored them as he walked with Kate.

"That's a good reason to live someplace."

He looked at her, and a hint of warmth seemed to finally reach his eyes as he answered. "I think so."

Just then, her phone rang. She dug it out of her pocket to see the word "Douchebag" flash across the screen in capital letters, along with Cody's number. She quickly hit the ignore button, but Javi had already seen it, and he roared with laughter.

She gave him a dirty look, but couldn't help the small smile that crept across her own face as she watched him.

"Okay," he finally said when he calmed down. "I'll admit it. I like you a little bit."

"Oh, be still, my beating heart."

That made him chuckle again, and he looked at her from the corner of his eye. "So, actor or surfer?"

"Surfer. Who used more hair products than me and screwed a bimbo in the back of the shop that mommy and daddy bought for him."

"'Douchebag' sounds about right then."

They walked in silence for a bit longer, then Javi nodded toward a food stand on the corner where an old woman flipped meat on a grill.

"This place has good tacos. You like tacos, right?"

"Who doesn't like tacos? That's like saying you don't like sandwiches."

"Exactly, but you should get the *tacos al pastor* here."

She squinted at him. "Are you always this bossy?"

Javi thought for a moment. "Probably."

He bought two tacos for both of them and brushed her away when she offered to pay, so she bought their drinks. They found a clean section of curb to sit along and she watched the passing foot traffic, wishing she had brought her camera.

"Wish you had your camera right now, don't you?"

Kate stared at Javi mid-bite, amazed he had read her so accurately.

"Yeah."

He grunted and muttered, "Just like Reed."

They finished eating in silence and she was surprised to find herself completely relaxed with the quiet man sitting next to her. She didn't feel the need to make conversation with Javi, because he clearly didn't want it, and Kate found the peace in the midst of the surrounding noise soothing.

"People aren't always the way they seem at first, Kate."

She looked at him, thinking about the surly sculptor she met at the warehouse, and about a reclusive photographer and a mysterious love. "No, I guess they're not."

"Did you love him?"

She coughed a little in surprise and took a drink of her soda. "The douchebag? Why do you want to know?"

He shrugged. "Just curious, I guess."

Kate smiled reluctantly. "Fair enough." She paused. "I thought I did. I thought I knew who he was. I thought he was a nice guy."

Javi snorted and shook his head. "The last thing *you* need is a 'nice guy.'"

She looked at him in shock and set her drink down on the sidewalk before she stood up. She didn't need a 'nice guy?' What the hell? Javi looked up in confusion, frowning at her suddenly angry eyes.

"You don't know anything," she choked out before she walked away.

She didn't hear him call her name.

PART SIX:
THE ASSISTANT

CHAPTER FOURTEEN

Corona, California
May 2010

Finding Brandon Wylie, Reed O'Connor's former assistant, did not prove nearly as difficult as Kate had imagined. In fact, after getting his full name from Vanessa before she left Los Angeles, a quick internet search provided her with his phone number, e-mail, and the physical address of Wylie Exclusive Photography in Corona, California, only thirty minutes from her apartment in Claremont.

He agreed to meet her for an interview as long as she bought him dinner and "enough beer to erase all memories of the Gonzalez quinceñera" from his mind forever.

And that was how Kate found herself sitting in a booth at the Outback Steakhouse with Brandon Wylie, alumnus of Foothill Art Institute and former assistant to acclaimed photographer Reed O'Connor. The years had invested Wylie with a sense of unfulfilled greatness, and he spent most of the dinner talking about his genius being wasted in wedding and family photography.

"Another 'Big Bloke,' sir?"

The friendly server looked at Wylie as the portly man shoveled another bite of steak in his mouth. He grunted in affirmation before quickly finishing the last few gulps of his enormous mug of beer. Kate stared wide-eyed and wondered just how much he would be able to eat.

"Miss?"

Kate tore her eyes away and looked at the young man waiting on them. "Another Coke when you get the chance?"

"No problem!" He hustled off to refill Wylie's beer and hopefully get another drink for Kate. So far, the meeting with Wylie had gone surprisingly well. He nodded appreciatively along with her as she explained her thesis project and drank his first beer. He peppered her with questions about the current happenings at his alma mater while he ate his dinner and drank his second beer.

While reminiscing with Brandon Wylie about Professor Potter's notoriously boring lectures or the finicky vending machine near the darkrooms was somewhat amusing, Kate was more eager to discover what insight he could give her into the enigmatic relationship between Reed O'Connor and Sam Rhodes. She felt a growing urgency to unravel the mystery of why the once devoted couple was no longer together.

According to Vanessa Allansworth, Wylie was the only assistant that O'Connor had employed on a regular basis, and the only one he had used at all once he started doing portraits full-time. Kate was curious why the reclusive photographer had hired the ruddy-faced man to begin with and equally curious why he had fired him. According to Vanessa, Wylie was around the same age as O'Connor, but Kate thought he looked at least a decade older.

"So, Mr. Wylie—"

"Nah, you're buying me beer. You can call me Brandon."

"Thanks. I just wanted to let you know I'm not publishing anything about Mr. O'Connor's personal history in my thesis. This is purely for research and my own understanding of his work. I have absolutely no plans to write anything—"

"Oh," he interrupted her, shrugging. "You can publish anything you want, as far as I'm concerned. I've got no loyalty to that asshole. What do you want to know?"

"Oh… okay. So, how long did you work for him?"

He sniffed noisily. "It was almost a year and a half, I guess? It was sort of a job-to-job thing at first, with the fashion stuff, then I worked for him full-time when he started doing portraits. I pretty much got stuck as O'Connor's errand boy. He didn't need my help with the portrait work as much as the fashion, but he kept me around to clean stuff up in the studio, get rid of curious people, run errands. Stuff like that. Then, after he got weird, he kicked me out of the studio altogether, and I just answered phones and did what Lydia—that's his agent—told me."

Kate leaned forward a little, one phrase catching her attention. "What do you mean 'after he got weird?'"

"Oh, come on," he snorted. "You must know his reputation. Trust me, it's well-earned. At first he was an okay guy. I mean, he was always an asshole, especially when he was working, but he kind of had a sense of humor about it. Then he…" Wylie trailed off, suddenly looking uncomfortable.

"What?"

He finally looked at her. "Fuck it. I don't owe that guy anything. He was totally messed-up over a chick. Not that you could tell by the company he kept, you know what I mean?"

"Not really. I've never heard about him having any company. All my research indicates the man is pretty much a loner," Kate said calmly, though inwardly, she was practically bouncing in anticipation at the unexpected treasure trove of information the former assistant had turned out to be.

"Oh, he doesn't anymore. That's probably true. No, when I first worked for him, he actually had a normal—well, sort of normal—girlfriend, if you can believe it."

"Really?"

"Oh yeah. Uh… Sam was her name. She was from around here somewhere, and they went to school together. She was a painter. Not that I know much about painting, but she was around. She worked in another part of the studio and was real private about her work, so I don't know if she was *really* an artist, you know?" He smirked as if sharing an inside joke.

Kate smiled back, amused that the photographer seemed to be unaware that one of the state's foremost landscape artists was the subject of his musing. She prodded him a little.

"So, this painter… was she the one O'Connor was messed-up about?"

Wylie nodded, frowning before he took another large bite of steak. He hadn't finished chewing when he continued. "Yeah. I never really got it. I mean, don't get me wrong, she was hot. Blond, pretty brown eyes. Total girl-next-door hot, if you know what I mean."

He took a gulp of the beer the server had just set on the table. "She had a nice ass, too. No offense or anything."

Kate fought the urge to kick his knees under the table. "So she was hot? What was the big deal? I mean, O'Connor did fashion photography. He must have been surrounded by gorgeous women all the time."

Wylie nodded. "That's part of the reason I took the job. His agent is the one that hired me, to tell the truth. He didn't want an assistant, but she insisted. She said O'Connor didn't want 'a little New York shit.' Said he wanted someone normal. I'd just graduated from Foothill and moved to New York. I guess someone at the college told her I was around." Wylie shrugged.

"So you got the job because... why? You were a Foothill grad?"

"Probably. The guy's fucked up, but he's got school spirit or some shit. Lydia told me once he set up this huge scholarship at the college with some money his dad left him. Totally anonymous. He didn't live rich, so I guess you'd never know, but I think he was pretty loaded."

"Really?"

"Oh yeah. And I bet he's *really* loaded now, with all the celebrity portraits. Those have got to pay good. But for the first year I worked for him—before he broke up with the girlfriend—he was like a hermit. He had a few people that hung around, but it was mostly just him and her... and his agent, I guess. But they never went out, or at least, not much. Openings every now and then, when one of their friends was showing and they had friends visit from California sometimes."

Kate shrugged. "I don't know, he sounds pretty normal from the way you describe him. I don't know why everyone thinks he's such an asshole."

"Probably 'cause of the way he is when he's working." Wylie paused to wave the server for another beer as he finished the one he was drinking. "He was in his own world when he got in that mode. Fucking brilliant, but he didn't notice anything or anyone but the subject, you know? Maybe that's why he kept Sam around." He snorted a little. "She was like his guard dog—a little blond pit-bull!" Wylie laughed at his own joke before settling down again.

"A pit-bull, huh?"

"Yeah, she and I didn't get along very well. She was usually a super-moody bitch. She'd act all stuck-up most of the time, unless O'Connor came into the room, and then it was all about him, you know?"

"Really?"

"Yeah, I don't know. The sex must have been amazing or something, 'cause she was super jealous, too. With all the models and shit?" He shook his head and looked down at his almost empty plate. "I guess she had reason to be. I mean, I'm sure he was fooling around on her."

"Yeah? What makes you think that?" Kate asked with an incredulous snort, remembering Dee, Javi, and Vanessa talking about how dedicated and loyal the two were to each other.

"Maybe because he kissed a chick right in front of her after a photo shoot one time?" Wylie said. "Well, I mean, he didn't know she was there. He was in his 'work mode' and I guess he must not have heard her come in the studio." He waved his hand dismissively. "I saw the whole thing."

"What?" She felt her heart plunge, and her voice was barely audible in the crowded restaurant. Her mind rushed back to Cody's betrayal, and she swallowed the lump in her throat, determined not to lower her guard around the obnoxious man in front of her.

"Yeah, first time I ever really felt sorry for the moody bitch. She looked like she'd been punched in the gut. I thought she was gonna hurl on the equipment for a minute, and I'd have to clean it up."

Kate sat speechless, fighting the unexpected tears that wanted to come to her eyes. She felt a sudden urge to rip up every complimentary word she'd ever written about Reed O'Connor. "So, what—" She cleared her throat a little before continuing. "What happened when she saw him?"

"O'Connor turned around after a second, saw her, and started yelling at the top of his lungs for everyone to leave." He laughed. "Including the chick he'd just been kissing! I was the last one out, and I heard them start fighting. She was ripping into him, that's for sure. I was tempted to stick around, but I wasn't that interested in O'Connor's love life, you know? I guess they broke up."

"So, uh…" Kate swallowed thickly, determined to get as much information as possible from the interview. "You never saw her around again?"

"Nope. I turned up at his studio downtown the next day and everything was locked up. I kept coming by for a few days, but no one was ever there. I finally called Lydia, and she told me to just stay home for a while. Didn't hear a word from him for like… six weeks? Kept getting my paycheck, so I couldn't complain about that. Finally, he calls me up, tells me to be in the studio the next day for work and that was that."

Kate paused, remembering what the man had said earlier. "And that's when he got weird?"

He nodded dramatically. "Yeah, big time weird. He barely talked unless he absolutely had to. The fashion stuff sort of stopped. 'Course, maybe he just ran out of fresh models to screw, or after the girlfriend left, the thrill was gone. He did start banging new chicks about six months later, though."

"And then?" Kate said, her lip curling at the man's callous attitude.

"Then, if you can believe it, he got even weirder. He worked alone, mostly at night. I snuck in the studio one morning, and he was sleeping in the corner. Had the light kits set up at all these crazy angles. I could never figure out what he was shooting. 'Course, crazy must sell, because all the celebrities started showing up right after he and the painter broke up."

"Oh, yeah?"

"Yeah, Lydia sort of had to baby him at first, but for some reason, they all loved the guy. He was the hottest ticket in town all of a sudden. And the ironic thing was, O'Connor didn't give a shit about any of it."

Wylie smiled, but shook his head in confusion. "So, I worked for him like... half of 2005 and through 2006. Then right after New Year's, he sat me down and said he didn't really need an assistant anymore."

She felt wooden, going through the motions of the interview while her heart ached in disappointment.

"Were you pissed off?"

He grimaced. "To tell you the truth, I was sick of New York at that point. Too much drama. Shitty weather. Too damn expensive." He took a deep breath and finished his beer in one gulp as Kate stared at him sullenly. "I was ready to come home. Nothing beats SoCal, you know? Sun and surf, baby." He smiled with a satisfied grin.

"Yep," Kate said bitterly. "You've got it made, Wylie."

CHAPTER FIFTEEN

Brooklyn, New York
March 2005

The tiny Asian woman paced in the middle of the room, swinging her arms wildly as she tried to get through to her friend.

"You have to hire someone! This is getting ridiculous. You spend twice as much time on shoots as you need to because you refuse to hire anyone for more than a day. If you had a regular assistant, they would already know what equipment you liked, what lighting you prefer, and how to set everything up. Then, you could show up, do your work, and leave." Lydia threw her hands up at Reed's complete and utter disinterest.

He was sitting at the kitchen table in their apartment in Williamsburg, examining a contact sheet from his latest job. He moved the loupe deliberately across the page, oblivious to his agent's frustration.

"Argh!" Lydia rolled her eyes and sat down on the plush green couch Sam had picked out six months before when they finally found a decent-sized apartment. "Sam, help me out here. Wouldn't you like your boyfriend to work less hours?"

The painter, who was working on sketches for a series featuring street performers, refused to look at her friend and agent across the room. She sat at a drafting table, her pencil adding quiet background noise to the open room.

"Lydia, don't even try to draw me into this one. This is between you and Reed. I'm staying the hell out of it," she answered and continued sketching, turning a page in her book to capture the look of intense concentration on her lover's face as he worked.

They had been together for almost five years, but Sam continued to be fascinated by the subtle variations of expression that crossed Reed's face, particularly when he was working. They were still each others' preferred model for almost everything, though Sam conceded she had neither the patience nor the stature for the fashion work Reed had become known for.

He had been working much longer hours, but as always, if it didn't bother Reed, it didn't bother Sam. They both trusted Lydia implicitly with the management of their careers, and they were as fiercely loyal to her as she was to them. The agent did occasionally try to use their influence over each other to her advantage, as she was trying to do at the moment.

Usually, both Reed and Sam laughed it off. This time, however, the temperamental photographer looked at Lydia with irritation. "Lydia, give it a rest. Don't you have something to do? We're both trying to work here."

Lydia kicked her feet up on the small couch and settled in, tucking her long hair behind her ears and lifting an eyebrow.

"I know you are, but I have a date later. Hanging out with you guys when you're both working gets me revved up. It's like vicarious foreplay."

Reed only shook his head. He did, however glance over at Sam, who met his eyes with a sexy wink. Just Reed's eyes on her gave Sam a few ideas for how they might fill the time when they could finally kick Lydia out.

Lydia shivered. "See? Just keep eye-fucking each other like that. It's so damn sexy. Speaking of your swirling sexual chemistry, how about some pictures or canvases of the two of you together? That would be stunning. I could sell the hell out of something like that. Tastefully done, of course. Or not," she mused. "I could sell either."

"No," they said simultaneously from across the room.

Lydia sighed. "I'll ask again tomorrow…" She trailed off before piping up in a more cheerful voice. "Hey, Vanessa's going to be in town next month for her show."

Sam smiled. "We haven't seen her in… How long has it been? Reed, do you remember?"

He looked up and furrowed his dark eyebrows in concentration. "Has she been here since we moved into this place?"

"I don't think so. I think we were still crashing with Lydia when she visited last time."

"Well, shit, it's been almost six months then," he said before returning to work.

"Hey, Reed?" Lydia called his name in a slightly sing-song voice.

"Yes, Satan?"

Sam snorted from across the room.

"Will you do Vanessa's pictures for her show? Pretty please? You have the time right now. I know your schedule." Lydia grinned slyly.

"Hmm. Imagine that. I *do* have time right now. How did you know?" He rolled his eyes. "Of course I'll do pictures for Vanessa. She's great in front of the camera. Does she need shots of her work too, or just publicity portraits?"

"Both. Dee has some pictures for me from the stuff she's seen, but if you could shoot the new stuff, that would be great. Her portrait's the priority though, and I'm hoping to do some cross-promotion for you both. I want something that screams 'mysterious and sexy,' all right? Nothing weird."

"I know how to shoot a portrait."

"Oh, I know you do, I just don't want—"

"I'll shoot her the way I want to, Lydia."

Sam smirked at the undercurrent of annoyance in Reed's voice.

"I just don't want to have to explain the irony of publicity photos featuring the painter's ear or something."

Sam pursed her lips, waiting for the fight their friend had started, whether she knew it or not.

Reed sat back in his chair. "Are you questioning my ability or talent?"

"No, I just—"

"Training?"

"Reed—"

"I'm sorry, has a client been unsatisfied with my work in any way?"

"Yes, but you usually just tell them to throw the proofs away and hire someone else. Which, of course, they never do."

"Because I know what I'm doing better than they do, which is why I will shoot Vanessa *exactly* the way I want to, Lydia. And you'll like it, or you won't ask me to do another freebie portrait for you—ever. Got it?" His voice was dripping with irritation, and his blue eyes glared at the agent.

Lydia glared back. "Fine. Just remember, I do all this shit for you guys. And none of you have to worry one bit about marketing, or little things like—oh, I don't know? Selling the stuff you produce? So don't pull the artistic temperament bullshit with me, Reed."

Sam frowned as she felt a twinge in her lower abdomen. She stretched her arms up, hoping the sharp pain on her right side was caused by the angle at which she was sitting. Unfortunately, as she stretched, the pain grew worse, and she swayed a little, dizzy even as she sat on her stool.

Reed's eyes cut to her immediately, forgetting the argument with Lydia. "Sam? Are you okay?"

The painter stood up slowly. "Just a cramp, I think." She waved her hand dismissively as she walked over toward Lydia on the couch. Her friend eyed her, noticing how pale she was and the slight tremor in her hands.

"Sam, honey, did you forget to eat today?" Lydia asked cautiously. She had to force her to eat sometimes; Sam would forget after days of working on a canvas. Yet despite the lack of sleep and poor diet, Sam was almost never ill.

Reed stood, forgetting his work on the table and striding toward her. Sam saw the frightened look in his eye an instant before she passed out.

Hours later, she lay silently in a hospital bed after emergency surgery, painfully recalling the panicked ride in the ambulance and the confusion in the emergency room. She curled into herself on the narrow bed, taking shelter in the dark room and the feel of Reed's hand as it cradled her own. He was sleeping in the chair next to her, pulled up close to her bed.

"Are either of you a relative?" the doctor asked.
"I'm her boyfr—"
"I'm her sister," Lydia broke in, ignoring the doctor's incredulity over the obvious lack of resemblance. "What's going on?"
Sam lay next to them, trying to focus on anything but the pain as she felt the drugs they injected slowly start creeping through her system. She clenched her eyes in agony.

The doctor cleared his throat, but his words began to cut out as Sam slipped more deeply under the influence. "—your sister… symptoms of an ectopic pregnancy—"

"Hard to know how far along…"

"—too late to use medication to clear—"

"Sir?" She finally heard clearly. "Sir, are you the father?"

"The father?" Reed repeated in a crushed voice. Sam lay there, anguished from the pain she heard, wishing she could hold him and protect him, but unable to move as the anesthetic cloud covered more and more of her mind.

She didn't remember anything after that.

Sam looked at him lying hunched over in the dark hospital room with his head by her thigh and his hand holding her own. She reached over to stroke the soft hair he had let grow out over the past year just because she liked it. She squeezed his hand and thought about all the times over the years she had sketched them. He was so beautiful to her. She felt the tears roll down her face at the thought of the lost child they hadn't even known they'd created. What would he have looked like?

She heard a baby cry down the hall, and she sniffed. Reed's head shot up, looking around the room in shock, before he saw Sam lying on the bed. His tired eyes tensed, and he reached a hand up to cup her wet cheek.

"Are you hurting? I'll get a nurse. Don't cry. It's going to be okay. I'm sorry. I'm so sorry, Sammy."

She sniffed again, wiping her eyes with the edge of the sheet that lay over her. "Why are *you* sorry? I'm the one who didn't even realize I was pregnant. So stupid… it's probably my fault. You're always saying I don't take care of myself enough," she muttered as she tried to staunch her tears.

"Don't. It's no one's fault, okay? The doctor said there could be a million reasons this happened." He exhaled a shaky breath. "Sometimes shit just happens. You're going to be fine." He stood and leaned over, pressing a kiss to her forehead and holding her cheek in his hand. "You're going to be fine. That's the most important thing. That's what scared me the most. I was so—" Reed choked. "I thought I was going to lose you for a while." He leaned over her hospital bed so he could hold her head to his chest as he squeezed her limp hand.

Sam let the tears fall, finally allowing her body to shake with sobs as Reed held her in his safe arms.

"I wish I could lay down with you." He stroked her cheek. "It's so cold in here."

"It's okay. I don't really feel it."

After her tears had dried some, Sam lay back, reclining on the bed and watching Reed as he sat next to her. He was obviously exhausted, but he traced his rough fingers up and down her arm with the lightest of touches. The feel of his skin on hers seemed to soothe them both. His voice finally broke the silence.

"You know I'd never leave you alone if you were pregnant, right? You know I'd love our baby, too?" he asked hoarsely, his eyes tracking his fingers as they continued to trail up and down her soft arm.

She reached over with her other hand, tangling her fingers in his shaggy hair. "I know, Reed. I've never worried about that."

"Just wanted to make sure." His left hand reached up, and he wove their fingers together as he lay his cheek down on her thigh and stared into her brown eyes. "I love you so much, Sam. I don't know what I'd do if I lost you," he said in the dark room.

She stroked his stubbled cheek. "Sleep. I'm here. I'm not going anywhere," she whispered as he closed his eyes. "Just look for me in your dreams."

"I always do," he murmured as he drifted off to sleep. "Always."

CHAPTER SIXTEEN

Newport Beach, California
June 2010

Kate sat on the deck of her parents' home, watching the sailboats as they left the harbor. Though the day was likely to be warm, a high fog still hung over the coast, keeping the sun at bay. She was thinking of taking her camera down to the harbor to take some pictures, but had second thoughts.

It all seemed so unbearably sterile. The boats were perfectly painted and washed. The docks were scraped free of mussels and barnacles. It was the ideal setting her parents had worked so hard for, but she suddenly found it as empty as the minds of the tanned girls who giggled as they posed on the bows of passing luxury boats.

"Hey, grumpy." Her father came out to the deck and sat next to her as she stared off into the distance.

"Hi."

They sat in silence for a few minutes, watching the boats, the water and waving to a few neighbors who walked or floated by.

"Why did you drive all the way out today if you're in a mood, Katie?"

"I'm not in a mood." She glanced at him as he sat with an amused expression on his face. "Fine. I'm in a mood. Mom's driving me crazy with this Cody stuff."

He smiled ruefully. Derrick Mitchell had years of practice running interference between the two stubborn women in his life. While they shared the same delicate beauty, Katie and Shannon Mitchell typically came from opposite ends of almost any issue most days. Her father was usually the one caught in the middle.

Her dad rubbed her shoulder soothingly. "She means well, Katie-girl."

"Does she not see that Cody and I aren't going to happen? Seriously? Why does she even want me to see him again? If she caught you cheating on her, you know she'd kill you."

"But not before mutilating me first," he pointed out. "You know, you have to remember that she's still remembering that darling little boy you grew up with. Cody's her best friend's son, and she's had this dream of you guys getting married with the big wedding and giving her adorable grandchildren. She's had that dream for years; you're going to have to give her time to let go of it."

Kate started to speak, but her father interrupted her. "Your mom didn't see the reality, and she's still coming to grips with it. And to tell the truth, you don't seem all that upset to her."

Kate's mouth dropped open. "I'm not upset? I—"

"Got your pride hurt. Which is understandable. But if you're feeling some deep loss over your relationship with Cody, you're hiding it. Very well," he said quietly. "And if you are, that's understandable, too." He paused and watched as Kate turned back to watch the boats as the sun began to peek through the fog. "Just give her a little while. The first time she sees Cody with some other girl, she'll turn into a mama bear, and then he'll be the one scared."

Kate muttered, "I don't ever want to see him again."

"Well, it's not likely you'll be able to avoid him completely, is it? Carl and Barbara are still our best friends, though I've never approved of how they spoiled their son. They're still good people, and I know for a fact they adore you." He patted her arm a little. "This is going to come bite him in the ass. Don't doubt that for a second. But I'm going to be honest." Derrick paused until his daughter looked at him. "You're better off without him."

She looked away as the tears welled in her eyes.

"I know it hurts now, but you're too bright. He never really understood you. Heck, *I* don't understand the way you see the world sometimes, but I'm smart enough to know you need

98

someone who gets that about you. And he didn't. More, he was never going to, no matter how much your mom loved the idea."

They sat next to each other for a few minutes, content to sit and watch the boats pass. Finally, Kate decided to change the subject. "So you know that photographer I'm doing my thesis on? I guess Professor Bradley and Dee are friends with him."

"The famous guy?"

"Yeah." She nodded. "They went to school with him."

Her dad sat up, his face lit with enthusiasm. He had never really understood much about photography, but Kate's dad had always been her biggest fan. "You should ask them to set up an interview or something, Katie. That'd be great for your thesis, wouldn't it?"

She shrugged, and her father frowned at her unexpected lack of enthusiasm.

"I think I have enough for the written portion."

Derrick snorted. "Says the girl who graduated a year early and begged the art institute to let her live on campus at seventeen." He frowned. "Since when has 'just doing enough' been good enough for you?"

Kate remained silent, wondering why she had brought up O'Connor with her dad when she really didn't feel like talking about the philandering asshole anymore. She'd tossed around the idea of changing her thesis topic, but knew it would be self-defeating and immature. She mostly wished she wasn't still curious about Reed O'Connor and his relationship with Sam Rhodes. She couldn't get past the feeling that there was something she was missing, and Kate hated the contradictory feelings she had about the whole subject. Was Brandon Wylie lying? Why would he? But if he was, what could have broken a relationship that seemed so strong to all of their friends?

"Why do guys cheat, Dad?"

He shook his head. "Oh, Katie… Sneaking around never made much sense to me. But then, I've never seen the point of putting time and energy into betraying someone you're supposed to love instead of using that time and energy to make things better."

She sniffed a little and cleared her throat. "Yeah. Me either."

"Besides, I'm a really bad liar. Your mom would catch me."

She laughed as she looked at her father's eyes, which were crinkled in amusement. "Yeah, you are. That's a good thing, you know?"

"I never said otherwise. That's the part that bothers me the most about Cody. The lying. Everyone deserves the truth."

"Yeah." She nodded slowly. "They do."

He grabbed her hand and squeezed it. "Not all guys cheat."

Kate looked at her father and thought about her parents' marriage. As much as her mother may have driven her nuts over the years, she had never seen a couple more devoted or fiercely loyal to each other as Derrick and Shannon Mitchell. They had been married for almost thirty years.

"I know, Dad."

He leaned over to kiss her cheek. "The right one will know he has a one-of-a-kind girl with you," he said quietly before he walked in the house. "I know it. So don't settle for less."

Kate heard her phone ring from the pocket of her jeans, but she didn't feel like talking to anyone, so she let her voicemail pick up as she stared over the quiet water.

Pomona, California

Javi Lugo hung up his phone as he sat at the kitchen table at his sister's house. He tapped it thoughtfully and wondered for the hundredth time why he cared whether he hurt the feelings of the little redheaded photographer.

"Javi, can you go get the boys for dinner?"

He could smell the *chile verde* Marisol had made from their mom's recipe, and he wondered again how she managed to make it so perfect. Maybe it was genetic. Brown hair. Brown eyes. Ability to make the perfect dinner. That trait had obviously skipped him. The spicy smell of pork, green chiles, and cumin wafting from the small kitchen would probably always remind him of his childhood and Saturday afternoon dinners with his family when he was growing up. He wondered what smell reminded Kate Mitchell of home. Probably not *chile verde*.

"Javi?"

"Yeah, I got it. I'll get 'em."

He shook himself from his reverie and stood up, glancing at the number on the screen one last time before he pocketed his phone and went to corral his unruly nephews.

"Manuel? Robbie?" Javi called as he walked down the hall toward the noise. He walked into the boys' small room, decorated in the cheerful colors he had helped Mari paint when she first moved in, to see his older nephew holding down his little brother and tickling him mercilessly.

"Uncle Ja—a—vi!" Manuel panted. "I'm going to pee my pa—pants!"

"Get off your brother, Robbie. If he pees, you're cleaning it up." Javi flicked the six-year-old's ear and pulled them apart. "Dinner's ready. Go wash your hands."

He was trying to be better about spending time with his sister and her boys. She had, after all, moved out to Pomona to be closer to him after her crap boyfriend left her on her own with two kids the year before. Mari may have been twenty-eight, but she would always be his little sister, and he still felt a responsibility to take care of her and the boys.

Javi sat down to dinner, joining them in the quick prayer Mari offered before he began inhaling the *chile verde*, rice, and beans. He tried to remember when the last time he'd had a full meal was. If it wasn't for his sister, the small restaurant she worked at, and the taco truck near his warehouse, Javi realized he would probably never eat.

"Who were you trying to call before dinner?"

Javi looked at Mari in surprise. "What?"

"You kept calling and hanging up. Who were you trying to get ahold of? Your agent?"

"No, Lydia's in New York right now." He continued eating dinner, trying to avoid her question and stealing a tortilla off of Robbie's plate when he wasn't looking.

"So who was it?"

"Why do you want to know?"

She teased, "I don't know. You had a funny look on your face."

"No one, really."

Mari curled her lip. "It wasn't the painter, was it?"

Javi glared at her. "And if it was?"

"Nothing. I just don't think—"

"You don't get to think anything about that, Mari." He scowled and turned back to his food.

She stared at him across the table before she stood up and walked to the refrigerator to get more milk for the boys. Javi set his fork down, annoyed he had pissed off his sister, but not wanting to hear her opinion on his on-again-off-again relationship with Vanessa Allensworth which he hoped, was finally "off" for good after their last conversation.

Javi and Vanessa were friends. They'd been friends for years. And sometimes they were more, but never as much as Javi wanted; and their relationship, whatever it was, wasn't something either one of them would acknowledge to their once close-knit circle of friends.

They'd had been drawn to each sporadically over the years, but had failed to ever find enough common ground to build a real relationship. They were both too stubborn. And he had realized, as he was finishing up the necklace she'd asked him to make for her that he would never truly fit into her well-ordered life.

He'd made the jewelry out of white gold, as she had asked, even though a warmer metal would have better suited her skin tone. And she had asked for sapphires, though Javi always thought she should wear warm stones like agate or citrine. She frustrated him. In the end, he'd made it the way she wanted, but couldn't bring himself to deliver it to her, knowing he was so dissatisfied with the piece.

Mari came back to the table with a gallon of milk and refilled the cups of her squirming sons before she sat.

"Hey, Mari."

She eyed Javi warily. "What?"

Sorry, he mouthed silently, unwilling to speak the words aloud.

She shrugged and went back to eating, the gleeful chatter of the two small boys filling the silence between them.

"Uncle Javi?" Robbie asked.

"Yeah?"

"Who's K—ate? Kate."

Javi grimaced and looked over at his nephew who was holding the phone that must have fallen out of his pocket. The six-year-old had hit the buttons and the call history popped up, revealing Kate's name and number. Reaching across, Javi swiped the phone from Robbie's hand as Manuel giggled.

"Is she your girlfriend?" Manuel asked, breaking into a fit of giggles, even as his uncle popped him on the back of the head.

He glanced at his sister to see her sitting with a satisfied smirk as she rested her chin in her hand. "Yeah, Uncle Javi," she said sarcastically. "Who's Kate?"

He didn't say anything, but gave his little sister a pointed glare as he finished the last bite of food on his plate. He stood up at the tiny kitchen table, his bulky shoulders awkwardly filling the small room. He wiped his mouth and mussed both his nephews' hair before he grabbed his keys from the counter.

"I gotta go. See you next week?"

Mari shook her head at him, rolling her eyes. "Fine. Be mysterious. I'll bring by some food after work on Wednesday. Are you going to be doing the mad sculptor thing all week?"

"Yeah, I have a new project I'm starting, and I'm finishing up the big metal piece for that building downtown."

"Okay, we'll see you next Saturday at the boys' games, right?"

He nodded and reached for his wallet in his back pocket.

Need anything? he asked silently.

His sister shook her head, but mouthed, *Thanks.*

Giving them all a quick wave, he walked out to his truck parked at the curb. Pulling out his phone one last time, he looked at the call log and the small name on the screen. He hit the call button one more time, not surprised when it went directly to voice mail. He quickly decided he would say what he needed to say and be done thinking about Kate Mitchell.

"Kate, it's Javi. Listen… I think you misunderstood what I meant last week. Not that you probably care. Anyway"—he paused— "you seem like a nice girl and I'm sure you'll find a nice…"

He trailed off as he looked back toward his sister's house. Mari's ex had seemed like a "nice guy" too, but he'd never been able to handle his sister's quick wit and desire for something more. Mari had intimidated him. Ultimately, the boys' father had run instead of appreciating what he'd had. Javi bit his lip and began speaking into the phone again.

"You know what? Fuck it. Don't find a nice guy. You'd get bored, and he wouldn't know what to do with you. So… yeah, be pissed at me if you want, but you—you're one-of-a-kind…" He paused, unsure of what he was really trying to say. "So just find a guy that gets that, you know?" He rolled his eyes at the longest voicemail in history. "Or just ignore me, because it's none of my business, anyway. Bye."

He hung up the phone and walked to his truck, determined not to think about the girl with the fiery hair again.

Part Seven: The Potter

CHAPTER SEVENTEEN

Claremont, California
June 2010

Kate could hear the laughter through the front door of the Bradley's house as she raised her hand to knock. She'd been planning on slipping the progress report under the door in case the baby was napping, but the loud laughter inside gave her pause. Biting her lip, she rapped sharply on the dark red door. Dee answered with a bright smile on her face.

"Kate!" She pulled the younger woman into the house with a warm hug and a laugh. "I haven't seen you in weeks. How are you?"

Kate gave her a small smile before she replied, "I'm doing great. My classes are done. I'm almost done with the written portion of my thesis, and then I'll have my exhibition in the fall." She waved the papers in her hands. "I was just going to drop these off for Professor Chris."

Dee snorted, "Professor Chris?"

She rolled her eyes and shrugged. "It's my own joke. I feel weird calling him anything besides Professor Bradley, but he keeps asking me to call him Chris. It's my own weird compromise."

Dee laughed. "Professor Chris…"

She ushered Kate further into the house where a blond woman in her late thirties was sitting at the kitchen table making silly faces at Sabina. She looked up at Kate and Dee when they entered.

"So this is the brilliant Kate I keep hearing about?"

Dee nodded and threw an arm around Kate. "Yep, this is Kate Mitchell, Suz." The woman watched them with kind brown eyes. She looked familiar, somehow, but Kate couldn't place her.

"Kate," Dee paused. "This is an old friend of mine, Susan Rhodes."

"*Susan* Rhodes?" Kate's ears perked up at the name and she realized why the woman must have looked so familiar. Though she was older and had slightly different features, she could have been Sam Rhodes' sister.

"You were in the photograph," Kate said. "The one with Dee and Chris. The one Javi took. Are you… I mean, are you her sis—"

"Cousin, hon. I'm Sammy's cousin," Susan said. She stood and held out a hand to shake Kate's. "And I'm not that old, Dee. Sheesh." She elbowed her friend as Dee sat next to her and took the drooling baby.

Dee chuckled. "Suz is also a very talented ceramic and glass artist in Crestline. Her studio is just up the mountain."

Susan made a face. "Ceramic artist? Don't make me laugh. I'm a potter, Kate. Ceramic and glass artist sounds way too fancy to be referring to me." She laughed as she sat down again and took a sip from the steaming mug in front of her. "And it's very nice to meet you. Dee and Chris are very excited about your work. They both think you're really talented."

Kate smiled politely, finally remembering her manners. "It's really nice to meet you, too. I've, uh… I've heard your name from a few people while I was doing my research. I didn't know you were Sam's cousin, though. Or that you were a ceramic artist."

"*Potter*, really." Susan smiled. "I'm just a potter."

Dee threw an arm around Susan's shoulders. "That's right. Suz and I are the humble artisans of our little group from school. No fancy-schmancy *artistes* here, just poor working stiffs." Dee winked. "Do you want some tea?"

"Craftsmen, Dee. We're craftsmen… or crafts*women*, I suppose? Which sounds kind of funny, for some reason."

"I'd love some tea, thanks," Kate said quietly.

Dee got up to get Kate a mug, handing the baby to her for a moment. Kate bounced the baby girl on her knee, leaning over to place a small kiss on her dark curly head.

"So, Kate, Dee says you're doing your thesis on Reed's work? That's great. He's such a gifted artist. It's wonderful that he's inspired you so much," Susan said with a smile.

Kate snorted a little. "Yeah, he's brilliant all right." She continued watching Sabina smile at her as the baby girl drooled a little and grabbed Kate's chin.

Susan cleared her throat. "So, not the idol you thought he'd be? Found out he was human after all? Who'd you talk to? Brandon Wylie? That was the assistant's name, right?"

Kate stared at Susan for a moment before she looked back at the baby. She just shrugged, not knowing what to say.

She heard Dee speak behind her. "Never forget *who* is telling a story, Kate."

"So he's lying?"

Susan said, "I don't know what he told you."

Kate looked up, still bouncing the baby lightly on her lap. Sabina began to fuss and kick her legs. "You're Sam's cousin. So tell me, do *you* still talk to O'Connor?"

Susan's mouth lifted in the corner. "Reed and I were never very close, to be honest. Sam and I were more like sisters than cousins when we were children, but Reed has a hard time opening up to most people. We talk very rarely now."

"Oh yeah?" Kate asked with a slightly bitter smile. "I can see why you might not want to stay friendly with him, considering."

Susan cocked her head to the side and smiled. "Be careful making assumptions, Kate."

Kate looked at her in astonishment. "You know why they broke up, don't you? I mean, if you're as close as you say you are with your cousin, you *must* know."

Susan sighed a little as Dee sat back down at the table. She handed Kate her tea and picked up Sabina. Dee grabbed a blanket from the back of the chair and sat down, opening her blouse discreetly to feed the fussy baby.

Susan spoke again. "I imagine I know as well as anyone besides Reed and Sam why their relationship ended. Well…" She sighed. "That's probably not the best way to phrase it."

"What do you mean?" Kate asked.

"Nothing really ended, you know. They just broke up."

"Yeah," Kate said, her lip curling slightly at the corner. "I know."

"No," Susan murmured, shaking her head. "I don't think you do."

Kate stared at Susan for a few long minutes, watching her while she drank her tea.

"Are you sticking up for *O'Connor*?" Kate was incredulous. Susan cocked an eyebrow at her, and suddenly, Kate felt like the youngest person in the room. She realized that she sounded like an annoyed teenager. "I mean," she started, "I just don't understand how he could throw everything away. Everyone said what they had was so special."

"It was."

She swallowed the lump in her throat, refusing to cry. "So why would someone throw that away? I don't understand. They sounded so extraordinary." Kate halted, unsure of what she wanted to say, and not understanding how she had become so invested in two people she only knew by reputation.

"They *were* extraordinary," Susan said. Kate saw Dee nodding silently from the corner of her eye as she stroked Sabina's cheek. "And I don't know everything that happened," Susan continued. "It's really not my story to tell. I know the basics. But more importantly, I know that Sam doesn't harbor *any* bitterness toward Reed."

It was then that Kate realized tears had come to her eyes. She swiped at them, embarrassed at her own emotion. Susan just looked at her with understanding eyes.

"How?" Kate asked. "How could she—"

"Like I said, I don't know everything; they're both very private people and were always extremely protective of each other, even when they separated. But I do know that if anyone is aware of their own shortcomings, it's Sam. And she's one of the least judgmental people I know."

Kate was silent for a few moments, then she asked, "Does she still love him?"

The tears that sprang to Susan's eyes were quickly blinked away. "Didn't I say it earlier? Nothing really ended."

Kate took a deep breath. "But he—"

Dee finally broke into the conversation with a gentle voice, "Eventually, Kate, you're going to realize that sometimes in life, there isn't a good guy and a bad guy. Sometimes, even with the best of intentions—even with people who love each other—things can happen. We all have to take responsibility for our own actions. Good or bad."

Susan looked at Dee, still blinking away tears. "That's true. Very, very true." She nodded, before adding in a lighter tone, "I think it's thirty, right Dee? Isn't that when you're required to own up to your own shit?"

Dee winked. "Yep, that's what the manual said."

"I keep losing my copy."

"I don't think I ever got mine." The two women laughed at what must have been an ongoing joke.

Kate couldn't help but smile, looking back and forth between them. She wondered, as she observed their playful banter, whether the friendships she had in school would develop into the kind of friendship she saw before her.

The tension slowly dissolved as the conversation turned to family, work, and other mutual friends.

"So, I thought Javi would just meet you for coffee or something, but did I hear he let you walk through his studio?" Dee asked. "That's like finding the holy grail or a unicorn or something."

"Not that you could find anything in that place," Susan said. "Who knows, maybe that's where the unicorns are hiding."

"No, Javi would kill them and turn them into taco meat if they were."

"True." Susan turned to her. "But he let Kate past the fiery gate. Whatever could *that* mean?"

Kate fought the immediate blush that rose to her cheeks. "He... uh, he was nice enough to talk to me, but—"

"And it's so funny," Susan added. "I was talking to Toni last week and she mentioned she'd seen Javi at the Art Walk last month with a redhead."

Kate stammered as two sets of eyes turned toward her. "Oh, that was nothing, we—"

"Well, that would be noticeable," Dee interrupted. "You never hear about Javi with anyone, that's kind of—"

"Unusual."

"To say the least."

"Nothing's going on!" Kate felt like he was blushing from her neck to the tips of her hair when she finally squeaked out the protest. "Really, he was just returning some filters I left at his place, and he showed me around the Art Walk because I'd never been before, and we ate tacos because... well, I think that's the only thing he eats. But he really, I mean... he doesn't like me." She looked around at the amused faces of the other women. "Really."

"No, of course not." Susan shook her head. "Javi doesn't like anyone."

Dee nodded. "No, very antisocial. He barely speaks to his own sister."

Kate still felt like her face was on fire. "Nothing... *nothing* is going on."

Dee and Susan were both just smiling at her like she was the butt of some inside joke.

"So, Suz, what do you think? You know I can't go right now, want to drag Kate here to New York next month to keep you company?" Dee asked. "She'd be fun to hang out with and she might even like museums as much as you."

"Oh, I don't know. She's probably not interested in—"

"I've never been to New York!" Kate said, looking between Dee and Susan. "Are you joking?"

Dee winked at her, patting the baby who had fallen asleep on her shoulder. "I have a feeling there might be things in New York for Kate to discover. Things. People. Maybe a few answers?"

Susan smiled. "I'm game if she wants to. I'm stealing Carson's plane to go up there anyway. It'd be nice if it carried more than one person for once. Besides, she could meet Lydia. I think Lydia would like her."

"Lydia Collins?" Kate gaped. The wonder of the surprise invitation paled in comparison to the opportunity to meet the famed agent. "You think Lydia Collins would like me?" She wasn't modest about her work, but the prospect of meeting the renowned agent was enough to make a seasoned professional swoon, much less a not-quite-out-of-school grad student. She could only gulp.

Susan laughed again. "If you can charm Javi, you can charm Lydia. Besides, I think she's bored with her old artists. She could use a challenge."

Kate was still mulling what Susan had said about her "charming Javi" when she finally processed what the other woman was proposing.

"Susan, I'm really grateful for the invite, but I don't have the money—"

"I'm loaded, by the way. I married this insanely wealthy guy who has more money than he knows what to do with. Luckily, he thinks I'm charmingly eccentric." Susan grinned. "His family has a condo in Manhattan, so don't worry about paying for a place to stay or anything. It's fine. Just keep me company, have some fun, and see what happens. I love taking newbies to New York for the first time." Susan winked. "Besides… you never know who you might run into."

A huge smile of anticipation crossed Kate's face for the first time in weeks.

CHAPTER EIGHTEEN

Brooklyn, New York
New Year's Eve 2006

Sam sniffed a little as she curled next to Reed on the bed. They watched the fireworks and revelry on the small television in their bedroom and held each other. She stared blankly at the screen as the crowd in Times Square went wild.

"January would have been a really easy birthday month to remember," she said with carefully affected nonchalance. "Though, I guess it comes right after Christmas, so that's not so great." Her voice caught toward the end. "You'd have to wait a long time to get presents again, you know?"

Reed took a deep breath, swallowing the lump in his throat that always threatened to overwhelm him when she spoke of their lost child. "Sam—"

"I know." She stopped him and let out a quiet breath. "I know."

He remained silent, pressing her more tightly against his chest and wrapping her in his arms. He rocked her a little and kissed her forehead gently, brushing away the blond strands that had fallen in her eyes.

"I'm going to get better, Reed," she whispered. "Promise. This year I'm going to be better. I'm going to stop thinking about it so much, okay?"

Reed clenched his eyes in pain, ignoring his own tears as Sam buried her wet face in his chest. He sniffed a little and cleared his throat.

"You don't have to stop thinking about it," he said hoarsely. "I just want us to be able to move forward. You know that. We have a future together. I just—I don't want you to forget that part."

"I know."

They lay in stillness as the hours passed, holding each other as the clock struck midnight. In time, they both drifted to sleep in each other's arms.

In the early light of dawn, Sam felt him get up and sit on the edge of the bed, stretching his legs and arching his back to get the kinks out.

She stared at his naked body. His was the only human form she sketched anymore. For weeks after her surgery, she had seen children whenever she left the apartment, their small, sweet faces peeked from every corner of the city and filled her mind. The only way she could keep from drawing them constantly was to focus on Reed. So, she sketched his arms, his face, the detail around his lips, and the blue eyes that watched her with growing concern.

She hadn't worked on a canvas of any other person in months, though she had started work on an oil rendering of her favorite picture she kept tucked away in her grandfather's Bible. Dee had taken the photograph years ago and given a copy to each of them. Reed kept his in their studio.

"Where are you off to this morning?" she asked, enjoying the way the morning light crossed his back, highlighting the dips and shadows of his shoulder blades. Reed turned, a sleepy smile crinkling the corners of his eyes. He crawled over her in bed, tickling her ribs a little and rubbing his morning stubble along her neck as he grinned at her.

"Happy New Year," he whispered before kissing her mouth.

"Mmmm, you're quite the party favor." She smiled, reveling in his sleepy attentions and stroking his face. Reed usually liked to cuddle in the mornings, choosing to linger in bed with her unless he had to work. They would often start the day by making love before falling asleep for another hour or two. He chuckled at her sleepy smile before getting out of bed to throw on some clothes.

"I'm off to a shoot."

"On New Year's morning? Whose idea was that?"

"I know, right? Don't they know what a party animal I am?" Reed rolled his eyes as she laughed. He'd become notorious in fashion circles for *not* joining in the party lifestyle that so many of his peers enjoyed.

"Apparently some idiot designer is demanding authentic morning-after-the-bash atmosphere for his spring collection. They even paid some hotel to keep the mess after its New Year's party. It's completely ridiculous, but that's why they pay me the big bucks. I should be back in a couple of hours. Wylie's already there setting everything up."

Sam wrinkled her nose. "I'm glad you have an assistant, but I still don't like that guy. He's so… weaselly."

He shrugged. "We'll see. I'm trying to give him a chance to prove himself, and besides… he heels well."

Sam slapped his shoulder. "He's not a dog!"

"Oh, but he is," Reed snorted. "Really, Sam, he is. You should see him drooling after these models we work with."

"Oh yeah, that Brandon Wylie, he's an irresistible one, all right."

Reed shook his head. "I still can't believe you convinced him that Italian girl was into him."

Sam belly laughed at the memory of the assistant's enraptured face as he stared at the gorgeous print model who was trying to relate in broken English that she only wanted a bottle of water, and not a date. Sam still wasn't sure whether Wylie had understood the girl wasn't interested in him. She was positive the model had no idea, but both Reed and Sam had quietly laughed for weeks every time Wylie mooned over the beautiful Cecilia.

Reed may have made fun, but Sam knew who the models were really interested in. Her boyfriend was gorgeous and incredibly sexy when he was working; she knew that better than anyone. His intense concentration and focus were enough to convince more than one model that he secretly had a 'thing' for them. It had put him in a number of embarrassing situations, which Reed usually reacted to by becoming a huge asshole and wrecking more than a few egos.

He paused after he slipped on his jeans. "Hey, Sammy, after Vanessa's visit next month, why don't we go down to Savannah like you've been wanting to? We could take a whole week—just the two of us. I'll deal with Lydia. It'd be good to get away for a while. We, uh… we haven't been away for months."

They hadn't been away since she had lost the baby, but he didn't mention that. Sam looked at Reed and his hopeful expression. She nodded silently and he smiled.

"Sure."

"Yeah?"

"Yeah, that sounds fun. Great idea."

He nodded again, "We just need some time away, I think. Just you and me."

She smiled again as she watched him pull on a grey t-shirt. He leaned over and kissed her goodbye, whispering "I love you" in her ear and giving her a quick wink and a sly grin.

Sam smiled and waved goodbye as he left the apartment, ignoring the automatic tightening in her gut. She would never have considered herself an insecure person, but in the months since she'd had her surgery, Sam had become somewhat illogical about the number of gorgeous women who threw themselves at her boyfriend on an almost daily basis. She knew she was overreacting, but no matter how hard she tried, she couldn't seem to grab hold of her usual composure or confidence.

There were times since the previous spring that Sam almost felt like she was being held together by bits of string. She was emotional, broke into tears at the slightest provocation, and slept far more than she ever had in the past. She'd also lost an unusual amount of weight because she forgot to eat.

She hadn't realized until she lost the baby how much she treasured the idea of having Reed's children someday. Now, the doctors informed her it was possible, but would be much more difficult when they were ready to try because of the damage from the ectopic pregnancy and the resulting infection and surgery.

Sam shook herself awake, throwing on a robe and going to the small kitchen to make coffee. She heard the knock on the door just as she took her first sip. Frowning, she walked to answer it, wondering who would be visiting so early.

"Lydia?" she asked as she opened the door. "Since when are you up at"—She squinted at the clock in the kitchen— "nine in the morning on New Year's Day? In Brooklyn?"

Lydia swept into the apartment and collapsed on the couch. "Don't ask, just give me coffee."

She snorted at her friend and went to the kitchen to grab another cup.

"Are you the one that booked him for the crazy shoot this morning?"

She squinted at Sam as she thought. "Oh, the Von Rothenberger shoot? Yeah, that guy's nuts."

Sam chuckled. Leave it to Lydia. She walked over and set the coffee down on the end table before she settled down to work in her sketchbook.

"Sam?" Lydia asked as she dozed on the couch, completely ignoring the coffee Sam had brought her.

"Lydia?" She was sitting at her drafting table, fidgeting with a charcoal sketch she had started in the subway the other day. It was the closest she had come to drawing people in months, and the toes of the busker peaked at her from behind the open guitar case strewn with coins.

"When are you going to let me put together a show with all your canvases of Reed?"

Sam smiled at the familiar question. "Mmm, let me think. Probably... never."

"Sammy?"

"Yes, Lydia?"

"You realize that straight women and gay men would gather from the four corners of the earth to attend that show, and pay ridiculously high prices for any of those canvases of your gorgeous boyfriend, right?"

She smirked and glanced up at her friend and agent.

"Yes, Lydia."

"Think about it, we would both be set for life."

"Still no."

"Selfish bitch . . ." she heard Lydia mutter, but Sam just smiled.

"Sam?"

"Lydia?" she answered drolly.

The agent was silent for a long moment, and Sam continued sketching, her head cocked to the side as she examined the edge of the guitar case on the paper in front of her.

"You know how much he loves you, right?"

Sam's fingers fumbled for a moment and the charcoal fell from her careful grasp. She stared at the unfinished detail on the frayed case.

"Yes, Lydia."

Her friend's voice was uncharacteristically hoarse when she spoke again. "He's really worried about you, Sammy."

Tears fell on the paper in front of her, magnifying then washing away the rough threads of the stitching she had sketched so carefully the day before.

"I know."

CHAPTER NINETEEN

Claremont, California
June 2010

"So... yeah, be pissed at me if you want, but you're—you're one of a kind, so just find a guy that gets that, you know... or just ignore me because it's none of my business anyway. Bye."
Kate listened to the message left by the surly sculptor for possibly the twentieth time. It hadn't escaped her notice that he hadn't called again, but—to be fair—she hadn't responded to him, either. She was strangely touched by the brusque voice mail. She knew Javi meant well, but she was still confused about what, exactly, he was trying to say.

Added to that, she found herself confused by her own mixed feelings for the man. She tried to brush off her curiosity about him as artistic interest, but her thoughts weren't lingering on the larger than life steel sculptures he created and displayed, and she couldn't stop wondering about Susan Rhodes saying she had "charmed" him. Much to her irritation, she found herself getting nervous at the thought of calling him back.

She'd woken in the middle of the night with an idea for a series of self-portraits, excited about the project until she realized the person who would best be able to help her was the sculptor whose message she hadn't returned for weeks.

"Shit."

She picked up her phone. He probably wouldn't even answer. Taking a deep breath and trying to imagine speaking in her most professional voice, Kate dialed the phone number she had programmed in weeks before when he had called her the first time.

She heard his phone ring and ignored the strange flutter of nerves that grabbed her throat for a moment.

It's a professional call, Kate. It's just Javi.

Javi. The sculptor. Dee's friend, who relaxed her and unnerved her at the same time. Javi, the talented artist whose intense scrutiny threw her off balance the few times they'd been in contact. Javi, who seemed to see everything, even things she hadn't been able to admit to herself. She swallowed quickly as she heard the expected recording pick up, relaxing slightly as she began speaking.

"Hi, Javi. It's Kate. I, uh… I have this idea—I mean, I don't know if you'd even be willing to help me or how busy you are right now. I imagine it's kind of presumptuous, but—"

She heard her phone beep and knew instinctively that it was him returning her call.

Shit, shit, shit!

She had to answer. He'd know from her message that she was the one calling. Taking a deep breath, she clicked over.

"Hello?"

"Katie?" A deep voice, rough from sleep, answered her. She gaped, suddenly unsure of what she wanted to say.

"Javi?"

Of course it's Javi, you idiot.

Kate heard him take a breath and exhale. "Yeah?"

"Did I—did I wake you up?"

There was a pause. "Yeah, I guess so. I—" He cleared his throat. It worked a little bit, but his voice was still a rough growl that sent a shiver down her spine.

"I've been working for a few days." She heard him release another deep breath. "Hmmm, what time is it?" he murmured.

Her heart rate picked up. She had woken him, and a picture of him lying bare-chested in bed leapt unbidden to her mind. She had only peeked at the intriguing tattoos that covered his thick muscles, but somehow in her mind's eye, she saw his richly decorated chest and arms laying against a white background as he spoke to her.

"It's… uh, it's around eleven in the morning." She swallowed and willed the image away. "On Thursday. I was just going to leave a message for you. I figured you'd be working." She squirmed, still trying to erase the mental picture from her mind as he replied.

"Well, you've got me now. What did you want?"

"I—um, you know, just call me back when you get a cha—"

"I'm awake now, Kate," he voice was clipped. "What do you need?"

You. She almost said it before thinking. *Wait, what?*

Kate finally blurted out, "I have a project I was thinking you might be able to help me with! It's a series of self-portraits. I know it's kind of presumptuous, but you have some things at the warehouse—"

"Yeah sure," he answered quietly before she could finish her thought.

"—and they—what, really?" she said, shocked by his quick agreement.

She heard him let out a yawn into his phone, and she pictured his square, stubbled jaw stretching with the sound. He didn't reply to her question, so she continued. "Listen, Javi, I got your message and—"

"Then you got my message," he interrupted, suddenly sounding more awake. "I said what I wanted to say. What time?"

"What? I mean, I just—I didn't mean to ignore you when—"

"Yeah, you did, or you would have called me back. Listen, Kate, my hair's too short to braid. I said what I needed to say. As far as I'm concerned, there's nothing else to talk about. I can probably help you with this project, if you want."

Kate nodded into the phone silently, even though she was alone in her small apartment. "Um, okay. Thanks."

"I'll be at the warehouse tomorrow morning around eight. Come whenever," he said. "I'm going back to sleep now."

"Okay. Thanks, I'll see you tomorrow."

She could have sworn his breath caught a little when he answered, "Bye." Then he abruptly hung up.

Kate sat at her small table in the kitchen, staring at her phone for a few moments and wondering why her heart was still racing.

Pomona, California
June 2010

Javi saw her small silver car pull into the warehouse the next morning a little after eight o'clock. He sipped his coffee and watched her through the small window near the kitchen. She got out, then reached into the car to grab her camera case. He bit back the groan when he saw the bare length of her legs. She walked toward the door of the warehouse, which was cracked open. He couldn't help but notice how the morning light caught her red hair, and he brushed a hand over his face, trying to clear his mind.

"Too young," he said, pulling his eyes away from her. "Too pretty. Too damn breakable."

He hadn't been able to sleep after she called, so he'd worked on some projects around the Craftsman house in Lincoln Heights he'd bought the year before and was restoring in his spare time. He worked on sanding the woodwork in the front dining room until he could hardly keep his eyes open, trying to fathom what had possessed him to offer the use of his warehouse to the distracting girl.

He could hear her picking her way through the maze of materials and equipment that littered the large space. He'd turned his usual punk music off that morning, in favor of the moody sounds of slide guitar. He went to sit at the small table, still drinking a cup of coffee from the donut shop while he paged through the local paper.

Javi glanced up as she drew nearer, examining her before returning his eyes to the story about halted residential developments. She was wearing a pair of cutoff denim shorts and a small blue tank top. His eyes lingered on her legs, wondering how they had remained unmarked as she stumbled through the cement blocks, rebar, and sheet metal that littered his space.

"You need better shoes in here. Boots or tennis shoes or something. I'd rethink those shorts, too, but they're your legs."

She ignored his barking orders and set her camera bag down as she sat across from him. "Good morning to you, too. No Sex Pistols today?"

He grunted, "Not exactly the best thing for a hangover."

"I like Iron & Wine, too."

Of course you do. He brushed a hand across his face and exhaled. "Goody for you. So, what's the project?"

Javi was never a fan of small talk, so he appreciated when Kate immediately launched into a description of what she wanted to do, which involved posing herself in various parts of the warehouse. She wanted the ruined, industrial look as a background, and thought the light would be easier to control indoors. As she elaborated on what she wanted to accomplish with the series of self-portraits, Javi allowed his mind to wander, knowing that he would agree to pretty much anything she wanted.

Just keep talking so I can watch your lips.

He'd thought about Kate Mitchell far more than he should have in the past month. In fact, ever since the phone call at his sister's house, Javi had been forced to admit that his interest in her was decidedly nonprofessional.

"—I'm going to New York in a couple of weeks with Susan, but if I could get started before I go—"

As he listened to her explain her goals for the project, Javi found himself fascinated by the distinctive curve of her lips and the contrast of the rose hue against her pale skin. She had a sprinkling of freckles against her nose and cheeks as if tiny sparks had sprayed against her skin, marking her.

Where else do you have freckles, Katie?

He scowled. Javi was frustrated by how attractive he found her. Kate's hair reminded him of a flame, not the sharp, hot flame of the welding torch, but the cooler diffused flame of the annealing torch he used for silversmithing, which heated a piece of silver to red-hot, only to let it cool to its softest, most malleable form. His imagination suddenly provided him with a vivid picture of how her hair would look spilling down her pale back.

How far would that hair fall? Would it brush across…

He forced himself to concentrate so he could listen to what she had planned.

"—making myself a part of the framing instead of the focus, though, at times that would shift. Of course—"

He realized it would be sheer madness to imagine she could be as attracted to him as he was to her. Kate Mitchell was beautiful in a way artists dreamt of. She was also young and, he was fairly certain, inexperienced. He, on the other hand, was in her own words "brutish-looking," twelve years older, and carried more tattered baggage than the thrift store down the street. While Javi wasn't a self-conscious person, he had no illusions about his own desirability.

"—and because you have such a variety of materials in the warehouse, I wouldn't need to worry about using things and then having them lay around or go to waste, because—"

Javi watched her with a measured gaze, more careful than ever not to give away his own interest. What had he been thinking, offering his warehouse to her? Not only did he like to be left alone while he was working, it would be a strange sort of torture to have to see this distracting creature in every corner of the space he spent the majority of his waking hours.

All those surfaces...

Javi refocused on what she was saying and was reminded why he found her so enthralling and why, in the end, he knew he would have offered her anything she asked.

Kate was brilliant.

But even more... she had guts. Her vision reminded him of Reed's in its clarity, but with an entirely different focus; and she had an openness and vulnerability his friend had never allowed himself in his own art.

"—so I really think with the variety of materials you have here, it would be ideal. I know this is your workspace, and I would totally understand if you didn't want me here, so please believe me when I say I wouldn't be offended at all if you say no or change your mind. I would totally understand... Or if you wanted to work out some sort of schedule with me so I don't bug you while you're working!" She leaned forward with a hopeful smile that almost knocked him over. "That would be fine, too. The layering idea I have means that I would need to do a number of shots over a time, so—"

"Yeah, it sounds fine, Kate," he broke in abruptly, suddenly desperate to escape her presence.

"Really? Do you want to work out a schedule or anything?"

"Uh... no." He cleared his throat. "Actually, I think it would be better if you only worked here while I was in the building. I know you're a friend of Dee's, so it's not like I don't trust you around my stuff. It's just, on the off chance that something shifted or... yeah. I just don't like the idea of you here by yourself if you might need help or got hurt. It's, you know, like an insurance thing."

Javi, you're an idiot.

"Oh." She looked shocked. "I hadn't even thought about that. I guess you're right. I mean, I don't have an assistant or anything, so—"

"I can keep an eye on you."

I'll watch you so much it'll probably drive me crazy.

He shrugged and tried to look disinterested. Javi noticed a slight flush color her cheeks when he glanced at her and wondered if he had inadvertently offended her. He looked away to stare at his paper again.

"Okay," she said quietly. "Thanks."

He continued staring down, sneaking quick glances at her. "No problem. Why are you going to New York?"

"She blushed again and he clenched his jaw, trying not to stare. "Susan Rhodes invited me, and I've never been. She kind of implied that she might introduce me to Lydia Collins, which would be huge. She's your agent, too, isn't she?"

"Yeah."

"So that's why. And I've never been. I really want to go."

"It's crowded and the people are snotty." *And I want to walk through the sculpture garden at the Museum of Modern Art with you.*

"Well, I want to visit at least once."

"You going to try to see Reed?" *If that asshole takes you to MoMA, I will never speak to him again.*

"I'll ask," she said, "but I'm not counting on it. It would be great to ask him some questions for my thesis, but I'm sure he's busy."

Javi did nothing but grunt and continue looking at the paper. He had no idea what he was supposed to be reading, but he knew he was going to end up calling both Lydia and Reed before she left.

"Can I bring my stuff in? Is there a good place to store it?"

Javi waved toward the back wall, and the door to the small office where he kept some of his personal work. "You've seen the back office. Just put your stuff there while you're working. There's some old desks there. You can use those, if you want. There's plenty of room. It'll be out of my way."

"Okay," she breathed out, and a gorgeous smile finally crossed her face. "Thank you for this. I really appreciate it."

Her smile knocked the breath out of him, but he managed to choke out, "Yeah. It's fine."

"I'm so grateful. This is—it's the first time I've been really excited about a project since... well, I'm really excited about it." Her eyes darted away from his suddenly intense gaze.

Javier Lugo, you are a masochistic idiot.

He just stared at her, wishing he could convince himself to look away.

"You're welcome, Kate."

PART EIGHT: THE AGENT

CHAPTER TWENTY

Manhattan, New York
July 2010

"Your portfolio is… interesting."

"Is that a good 'interesting' or a bad 'interesting?'"

Lydia Collins glanced up from Kate's portfolio and then down again, flipping another page over as she perused the young photographer's work.

"I can't decide whether I like that you aren't intimidated by me," she mused, flicking a piece of lint off her cream suit. It may have been blistering hot in New York that July afternoon, but Lydia's jacket was free of wrinkles, her smooth skin was polished, and not a piece of her dark hair was out of place.

"I *am* intimidated by you. I'm just good at faking it."

They sat in the small conference room of the agent's office downtown as she thumbed through Kate's student portfolio with focused concentration. She smirked a little at the girl across from her. Kate sat as still as she could. She knew she had the nervous habit of tapping her foot, but she was attempting to curb the habit, so as not to appear uncomfortable.

After a while, Lydia closed the portfolio and scrutinized her, as if examining a piece of art for purchase. Dee and Chris had always spoken warmly about their friend, but like everyone else from their group at Foothill, they all spoke about the woman with a kind of detached respect, as well.

Lydia Collins, Kate realized, was the one who got things done. She was the business woman. And Kate may have been an artist, but she was enough of her father's daughter to realize that if she really wanted to be a successful photographer, and not end up working for a surf magazine or shooting weddings, she needed a Lydia Collins.

"You need me," Lydia stated bluntly, as if reading Kate's mind. "I think Chris and Dee were right about you. You're very good. You might be great; that remains to be seen. You're very young, but that can be an advantage, too. And you're pretty. As much as it may irritate me, that matters, too. I need to know what kind of life you want."

"Excuse me?" Kate asked, attempting to be polite as her heart raced in excitement.

"You don't need to be excused, you need clarification. Be precise."

Kate rolled her eyes, which made the agent's mouth lift in an almost imperceptible smile. "Fine, Ms. Collins. What do you mean by asking me what kind of life I want?"

"That's an excellent question, Kaitlyn. I like it so much, I'll even let you call me Lydia. I need to know whether or not you would be willing to relocate, for one. Southern California isn't a bad base to have, though, so we could work with that if you wanted to stay there."

"I hadn't really—"

"I need to know if you are willing to travel on a regular basis. I need to know what your goals are. Basically, I need to know where you would like to be professionally ten years from now, because that affects what kind of choices you and I make for your career in the next few years."

Kate stared at the brusque woman with her mouth gaping a bit in shock. "Does that mean you want to represent me?"

"Yes."

"Are you joking?"

She frowned. "I have a dry sense of humor, Kate, but it's not *that* dry."

"Oh my God!"

"Yes, well… yay." Lydia said, curling her upper lip into what might have been a smile.

"I can't believe this," Kate breathed out.

Lydia looked at her, frowning a little. "You're not a… hugger, are you?"

"Normally I am, but I can wait on that if you'd like."

"That would be best. You're staying with Susan, correct?"

"Yes. Should I call her or something?" Kate's eyebrows furrowed in confusion.

"No, but Susan has always been a hugger. Save it for her."

Kate could no longer hold in her excitement and she broke into a huge smile. "Lydia, I—"

"You're excited. I'm excited. We're all very excited. Now, where do you see yourself in ten years? You never answered me."

Kate stared at the tiny intimidating person, truly panicked for the first time since the meeting started. "Do I have to tell you right now?"

Lydia finally laughed a little. "No, but you do need to start thinking about these things soon. I'm not going to ask you to sign any papers right now, since you're a friend of the family, so to speak, but you do need to sit down and think about your future."

The agent's expression turned serious. "You have time. Finish your thesis. Graduate. You know a lot of working artists. Take advantage of their experience. Talk to them. If you have a significant other, talk to him or her, but you do need to make some decisions."

Kate nodded seriously, suddenly cognizant of the huge turn her life could take with only a few words. She felt as if a whole new world had opened up for her since she saw the snapshot in Professor Bradley's office, and she tamped down the feeling of panic that started to swell, choosing to focus on her excitement at finding an agent who wanted to represent her. She looked at Lydia and held out a hand to shake. "Thank you, Ms. Collins—Lydia. This is huge for me."

"Well…" Lydia shrugged a little. "Since we're being up front, I'll tell you—I'm bored. And when two of my favorite artists give me a personal recommendation, along with an old friend who I respect a lot, I pay attention." She sat back and relaxed a little in her chair. "I'm genuinely looking forward to working with you, Kate."

"Really?" she smiled. "Susan and Vanessa recommended me?"

"I don't represent Susan. She's just a close friend. Vanessa and Javier Lugo recommended you."

"Javi recommended me?" Kate was shocked, and she noticed Lydia raise a curious eyebrow.

"Indeed he did. He said you reminded him of Reed O'Connor, which is a fairly extraordinary statement for him. The jury is obviously still out on that one."

"Really?" She knew she didn't currently sound like the brightest bulb in the box, but she was shocked—and more than a little touched—that the sculptor had spoken so highly of her.

"I was surprised myself. Javi usually doesn't like anyone. I might have recommended he get his head examined if he hadn't started bitching about having to shave for publicity photographs immediately afterward."

Kate smiled. "Yeah, that sounds like him."

"Does it?"

She felt the heat rise in her cheeks as Lydia's mouth curled into a smile. Her eyes suddenly looked lively with interest, but she let the subject drop. They spoke for the next hour about jobs that might be options for Kate in the future. Lydia told her stories about some of the strangest photo shoots she had ever arranged, including one that featured no less than two dozen print models, a white tiger, and a standard poodle that had been dyed pink. Kate was laughing so hard she thought her stomach might hurt the next day.

Lydia said, "I thought Reed was going to strangle the poodle... or his assistant, one of the two. It would have been too bad about the dog."

Kate couldn't help the snort of satisfaction that erupted when she imagined Brandon Wylie wrangling a pink standard poodle in Times Square as cars passed by him, honking loudly.

Lydia watched Kate with a twinkle in her eye. "I'm looking forward to this; it'll be good to have some fresh blood around. We tend to get too caught up in our old gang sometimes. Too much history. Too much routine."

"I think it's wonderful."

"Do you?"

"Yes. You. Dee and Chris, Javi and Susan and Vanessa, and—well, Reed O'Connor and Sam Rhodes, of course. It's like you guys were some amazing artistic family or something."

She saw Lydia's eyes cloud over a little and she began to shuffle papers on her desk. "I suppose that's one way to look at it."

"So, does Mr. O'Connor still do fashion photography?" asked Kate, grabbing the opportunity to ask about him.

Lydia glanced at her before looking back at her desk. "No, he only does his portrait work. He was brilliant at fashion, though.

And it's very good experience for a photographer, even if it's not your passion. You should really consider—"

"Do you think I could meet him?"

Lydia spoke in a carefully level voice. "I very much doubt it."

Kate took a breath before continuing. "I'm sure you've heard I'm doing my thesis on his work, and how it's related to modern interpretations of beauty. I'd really like—"

"I very much doubt it, Kate." Lydia repeated with a warning in her tone. "He doesn't do interviews, and he rarely meets with people he doesn't know. He values his privacy." Lydia took a breath before continuing softly, "I know you've been asking about him. About them. I want you to know that I am not going to talk to you about Reed, Sam, or their relationship. As far as I'm concerned, it's none of your business. I don't care what Dee and Susan say." Lydia's voice was unyielding, and Kate felt her breath pick up a little.

"But, I don't want to publish anything. I'm just trying to understand—"

"It's none of your business, Kate."

Kate felt the frustration build on both sides of the mahogany desk as they stared at each other. Finally realizing she wouldn't be able to persuade the stubborn woman, she slumped a little in her chair.

"Everyone else talked to me," she said in a sullen voice.

Lydia cocked her head and her eyes were fierce when she responded, "Well, I'm not everyone else. You'll figure that out soon enough. And to tell you the truth, you sound a little childish right now."

"I just don't understand—"

"No, you don't!" she broke in. "Do you think this is some sort of—of soap opera? Some mystery or game? Why is this so important to you?"

Kate sat speechless, trying to put into words the strange connection she felt with the two artists. "I—I've studied Reed O'Connor's work for years. And there's something... I just want to understand it. And him. I want to understand—"

"What, Kaitlyn? What are you trying to understand?" Lydia no longer looked angry, but she did appear to be a little exasperated. "Why is knowing about *them* so important to *you*?"

"I just..." Kate felt her throat start to close and tears pricked her eyes. "Everyone—Chris, Dee, Javi, Vanessa, Susan—they all talk about them like they had this extraordinary love. The kind of love that inspires masterpieces."

She finally saw Lydia's eyes soften, and the agent said, "They did, Kate. They…" Lydia looked toward her office door as if she wanted to escape.

Kate felt the tears gather in her eyes, but she was determined to at least try to articulate what she was feeling. "That's the kind of love people look for their whole lives. The kind of passion we're all trying to capture when we pick up a camera, or a paintbrush, or a piece of clay. It's all just trying to capture what they had. And they lost it! And—and I need to know how they lost it, Lydia." A tear slipped down her face. "I need to know *why*," she said almost desperately.

She heard the door to Lydia's adjoining office open quietly, and the agent looked past her with alarm painted across her face. Kate brushed the tears from her cheek and turned to look over her shoulder. Then she gasped when her gaze met a pair of sad, blue eyes in a now-familiar face.

"It's okay, Lydia," he said as a soft smile touched his lips. "Hello, Kate."

CHAPTER TWENTY-ONE

Manhattan, New York
July 2006

Lydia rushed down the sidewalk, ignoring the sweat that dampened her jacket and ran into her eyes. As she turned the corner nearing Reed and Sam's studio, she replayed the phone call she had just received from Susan.

"Lydia, do you know what the hell is going on?"

"What are you talking about? I've been in Boston for the past three days."

"So you don't know why Sammy showed up here this morning looking like shit and not talking?"

Lydia's breath caught in her throat, and a dull dread began to fill her chest. "Have you tried calling Reed?"

"Of course I have! I can't get ahold of him. No one is answering at the apartment or the studio. I don't have his assistant's number." She heard the other woman sigh on the other line. *"We need to figure out what the hell's going on. Are you in the city? Do I need to have Javi fly up there?"*

Lydia dropped the files she had been holding and stood up, reaching for the spare keys the couple kept in her desk drawer. "I'm on my way right now. I'll call you in an hour."

"I'm worried about him, Lydia. You know how he gets—"

"I know."

Lydia unlocked the studio door, noticing the light hadn't been turned on in the small reception area. The assistant's desk appeared as messy as it ever was, and her heels echoed on the tile floor. A knot formed in the pit of her stomach as she walked to the back door leading to the workroom.

She opened it and immediately saw Reed sitting in the small kitchen located in the far corner of the studio. He wore a pair of jeans and a white undershirt, but his feet were bare as he sat cross-legged on the ground with his back against the cabinets. One hand was buried in his messy black hair, and the other clutched something close to his chest.

"Reed?" she called, as she crossed the barely recognizable studio. Broken and cut canvases and torn photographs mingled together, littering the floor. She saw dents in the walls, and Reed's light kits lay smashed in the corner near a raised platform covered with a rumpled white sheet. One of the lights flickered sporadically in the dim space.

"Reed?" she called again. As she drew closer, she saw him rock slightly, and draw his knees up toward his chest. Her stomach clenched at the sight of him. Something was horribly wrong. He didn't look like the confident, controlled man she knew. He looked... broken.

"Reed." She put a soft hand on his bare shoulder. "I need to know if you're okay." Lydia had her suspicions about what had happened based on the cuts evident on the canvases strewn around the room, but she wanted to make sure. "Are you hurt?"

Tortured blue eyes finally lifted to meet her own. They were red, and several days' worth of dark stubble covered his face. Reed was barely recognizable.

"I fucked up, Lydia."

She knelt down, drawing his tall frame into her small arms as he clutched her waist. She felt his tears soak her collar, though he didn't make a sound; his right hand still grasped something tightly to his chest. She pulled back, and he grabbed a towel from beside the sink to swipe across his face.

She held his hand in hers, trying to unfurl his long, callused fingers to make sure they weren't broken. His knuckles were covered in white powder where his fist had met drywall, and his cuticles, which were always cracked, were torn and bleeding. He finally relaxed his grip, and Lydia saw small pieces of a photograph flutter to the ground.

Her breath caught in her throat when Lydia realized they were pieces of the beautiful photograph Dee had taken of them in college. It was one of the few pictures they'd ever taken together, and the only one she knew Reed kept with him everywhere he went.

Reed frowned when he saw the pieces on the ground, and he leaned down, trying to gather them up again. Lydia put a hand on his shoulder to halt him.

He lifted his gaze to hers, and finally spoke in a soft voice. "I didn't mean to rip it. When I realized… It's all fucked up now. I can't put the pieces back together."

She covered her mouth to hold in a cry, but Reed's eyes stayed dry as he picked up the tiny pieces as if they were precious metal.

Lydia stood on shaky legs and looked around. As she took in the wreckage of Reed and Sam's combined work, her heart broke. Only Sam would ever take a knife to the scattered canvases she saw around the room. Though she could see evidence of Reed's temper in the torn photographs and broken lights, he would never have lifted a finger to damage Sam's work.

Lydia walked toward the storage room where she kept all her finished canvases of Reed. Despite their ongoing joke, Lydia had always known her friend would never sell them. Though she never said it, the agent knew the paintings were Sam's love letter to him. She painted him over and over again as the years passed, capturing tiny scars and subtle changes in her lover's body that only she would ever see.

As Lydia pulled the door open, she felt as if she had been punched in the chest. Tears finally fell down her face as she surveyed the devastation at her feet.

They were all ruined. Some lay on the floor looking as if they had been stepped on, and others lay broken against the walls, their frames cracked and splinters visible, poking out at odd angles.

In the far corner, she saw one painting that seemed intact, covered by a white sheet. She walked toward it and reached up to pull the sheet off the last intact canvas.

It was unfinished. Faint pencil marks were visible beneath some of the smudges of oil, but the outline was complete enough that Lydia could see it was a rendering of the torn photograph Sam had started months ago and never finished. It looked like a piece of abstract art; the angles of the bodies were clearly visible, but their arms reached around hollow bodies that would never be filled in.

She left the painting in the storeroom, re-covering it with the dusty white sheet before she walked back out to the main studio. Reed had moved to the small table where they often shared meals. He sat hunched over, pushing around the pieces of the photograph, trying to nudge them into some sort of order.

She sat down silently, and heard him speak in a hoarse voice.

"Did she call you?"

Lydia shook her head and spoke in a soft voice. "No. Susan did. She's in California."

He nodded, seemingly unsurprised. Lydia looked around the room, taking in the torn photographs of his lover. Pieces of Sam's face lay scattered around the room, creating the illusion of some strange black and white collage.

"Reed—"

"I kissed a model."

She stared at him in astonishment, stunned silent for a long moment.

"You mean she kissed you?"

"No. I kissed her."

"What? What the hell, Reed?" Lydia felt like crying again. "Wh—what were you thinking?"

He just shook his head silently and stared at the door to the reception room. "She walked in and saw me. She saw me kissing that girl on the platform. And the white sheets…" he whispered in an anguished voice as he leaned his elbows on the table, clutching his hair. "And the light was just like…"

Lydia cleared her throat, trying to pull herself together. "Reed, why would you do that? Why would you even—I know how much you love Sam. And you know how she's been lately."

He shook his head. "I know. It was so stupid. This girl was just there. And she was laughing at some joke one of the make-up people told. For a minute, it seemed so simple. She was happy. She was so *happy*. And I just… kissed her. And as soon as I did, I realized it felt wrong, but then I heard her. And I knew she saw." Lydia had to strain to hear him. His hands were clenched into fists. "It's broken, Lydia." He lay his head down on the table, defeated as he let out a shuddering breath. "It's so messed up. Everything's broken, and I'm so tired."

She moved to sit beside him, laying a hand on his back. After a while, Lydia felt Reed's chest rise and fall in a steady rhythm as he slept fitfully, his head resting on the scarred table.

Lydia rose and went to the kitchen to get a trash bag. She didn't know what to do with all the broken pieces of art; but she could at least clean up the glass in the corner where the lights had fallen. She worked methodically, stepping outside to call Susan and let her know what happened, as best she could figure it out. According to her Susan, Sam had asked after Reed, heard Lydia was going to check on him, and then fallen into an exhausted sleep.

Lydia worked for hours cleaning up glass, clearing off the platform, and picking up the smallest pieces of torn photographs and broken canvas. The larger pieces of both she placed in the storage room, not sure what Reed might want to do with them, but not wanting to throw anything away. She swept and dusted, calling various people to cancel shoots, and rearranging her schedule so she could take care of her friend.

Reed had been sleeping for almost three hours when she finally heard him sit up, knocking over a bottle of water she had set on the table next to him. The water spilled over the torn pieces of photograph before it dripped on the floor, and Reed stood up, staring at them in confusion before looking around the studio.

"Lydia?"

"Yeah?"

He rubbed his eyes, obviously still half-asleep and confused by her presence. "Where's Sam?"

Lydia swallowed the lump in her throat before she answered. "She's in California, Reed."

He looked around, confused before his eyes settled again on the scraps of the torn photograph. His fingers touched them and he collapsed in the chair, defeated. Tormented eyes met hers when he whispered, "It wasn't a dream."

CHAPTER TWENTY-TWO

Pomona, California
July 2010

The warehouse was empty without her.

Okay, it would never be *really* empty, but though Kate had done her best to remain unobtrusive over the previous four weeks, Javi had become used to her quiet presence as he went about his days. She slipped in and out of the warehouse like a cat. Sometimes, he would hardly know she was there, except for the odd six pack of his favorite beer that appeared in the fridge, or the uncharacteristically tidy kitchen.

He sat sketching at the table, distracted from his commission piece by the subtle curves of the design he was working on. It would work best in wood. Something light and very fine-grained. Basswood? Linden? He furrowed his eyebrows as his finger traced along a distinctly feminine curve he had drawn. His pencil paused for a moment before he threw it down and closed his sketchbook, frustrated by his preoccupation. His eyes landed on a lens cap she'd left on the table.

You're an idiot, Javi.

It was getting ridiculous, distracting, and Javi had no idea how much longer he would be able to stand it without lashing out at Kate for something that was entirely his own fault. He knew she didn't intend it, but her quiet presence in the warehouse had started to make him lose his focus. The way she muttered when she was thinking aloud. Her intense stare that caught him at the oddest moments. The little frown that grew between her eyebrows when she was concentrating. He had no idea what to do about his growing attraction to her, and it didn't look like she was leaving anytime soon. Why had he offered his studio to her?

Because you're an idiot, Javi.

His phone rang on the counter, and he went to pick it up, grabbing a beer from the fridge, even though it was only midmorning. Reed's name flashed on the screen, and he and he touched the answer button.

"Hey, man. How's it going?"

He twisted open the beer and took a long drink as his friend spoke from the other side of the country.

"Oh yeah? She's meeting with Lydia today?"

Javi paused again.

"No, I called her, too. Vanessa and I both. And probably Bradley. She's good— No really, man. The girl's got that... thing, you know? Kind of like you."

Javi laughed at his friend's sarcastic remark. "Well, if Lydia doesn't scare her off, maybe you *should* talk to her."

He sniffed and began strolling through his mess of a warehouse, enjoying the rare conversation with his oldest friend.

"I think... you never know, Reed. Maybe... how long has it been? I don't know, man."

He rolled his eyes as he spotted a small light kit Kate had left set up near a stack of rebar. He quietly began packing it away to put with the rest of her equipment in the back office.

"What? Yeah, I like her. She's a nice girl and a good artist."

Javi cleared his throat and scowled at the phone. "Yeah... sure she is. Shut up, Reed." He paused for a few more minutes and ran a rough hand over his jaw. "I can't just ask her out."

He walked to the back office with the light kit, almost tripping over a pile of concrete blocks Kate must have set up as a prop. He stopped to answer his friend's irritating question.

"What the—are we in junior high or something? You want me to pass her a note in homeroom?" He paused for a moment. "It doesn't matter okay? I'm not asking her out."

He yanked open the door the small room, noticing that Kate had set up a little office one of the empty desks left by the previous owners. Some of her work was spread out in binders and loose pages scattered the surfaces.

"I can't, all right? Besides the fact that she's gorgeous and I'm kind of an ogre, she's twelve years younger than me." He paused, not really listening to his friend's lecture on the other end of the line as he thumbed through some of the proofs Kate had set out. They were the beginning shots of the self-portrait series she was doing.

She was so beautiful. That wild hair just killed him. He scowled when he heard Reed's annoying question.

"Besides, she's too much like you. It'd be creepy. Like dating my best friend, only twelve years younger and with tits."

Javi snorted when he heard Reed's response. "Asshole."

He continued to look over her work, absently fingering a hair tie she had left on the desk, noticing the golden-red hair that had twisted in it. He scowled when he realized how much he liked seeing evidence of her scattered around the building.

"No, man... if she's meeting with Lydia this afternoon—I don't know. Maybe talking with her might help. Even if it's just you." Javi cleared his throat. "Besides, then you can tell me what you think of her, you know? That way when you give me shit, you'll know what the hell you're talking about."

He twisted the tie in his fingers before he put it in his pocket as he walked out of the room, shutting off the lights behind him.

"Yeah? That's good, man." Javi paused before he continued quietly. "Uh, no, I haven't seen her lately. Not for a while. Maybe Dee—"

He paused, listening to Reed's interruption. "Yeah... no, I get it... sure."

Javi walked toward the kitchen to grab a pack of cigarettes. "I will. Take care, okay?"

He stood in the middle of his kitchen for a moment, his heart aching for his friends. He'd tried over the years, but they were both so damn stubborn. And they still loved each other so damn much.

"Bye, Reed."

Sitting down, Javi picked up a cigarette and lit it before his hand reached for the pencil. Then he opened the abandoned sketchbook to start tracing again.

Part Nine: The Genius

CHAPTER TWENTY-THREE

New York City, New York
July 2010

Kate's first impression of the elusive Reed O'Connor in person was that he was very… quiet. And tall. His dark, curly hair was cut short, and she could see a sprinkling of silver at the temples. A dusting of stubble covered his jaw. He wore a simple pair of blue jeans and a white t-shirt. She somehow expected him to be wearing black, even though it was the middle of July.

After introducing himself in Lydia's office, he politely invited her to his studio a few blocks away if she wanted to talk privately. Giving Lydia a quick glance, she rose and left the office with the familiar stranger. There had been no anger on his face, only a quiet and sad kind of acceptance.

He walked brusquely in the summer heat, and Kate almost had to jog to keep up with him. He put on a pair of dark sunglasses and kept his head down as he walked in front of her, and she noticed that, despite his stature and handsome face, no one seemed to give him a second look.

They ducked into the dim exterior office of his studio, where an empty desk sat, holding only a box of tissues and a half-full pencil cup. Reed opened the rear door, revealing a large, naturally lit loft studio. She followed the quiet man inside and looked around. The left side had been walled off with dividers to create what could have been a small living area, and the right side had all the paraphernalia of a working photographer's studio. Light kits, chairs, and drapes were spread around in a strange sort of interrupted still life.

It was warm inside, though she could hear the soft gust of the air-conditioner. Kate lifted her eyes to the sunlight streaming through the windows of the loft. She was surprised to see so much natural light in the studio, as it created a less predictable environment to work with for a photographer.

He noted her eyeing the large windows and smiled.

"When we picked this place, I told Sam those windows were going to drive me crazy. Natural light can be so unpredictable." He chuckled. "She loved it though. She did most of her work here too, and she always liked having that light." He fell into silence again, and she saw him fidgeting with his keys and rubbing his jaw as he looked around the loft. He looked like he hadn't shaved in several days.

Kate looked around. "Do you live here now?"

He frowned. "I have an apartment in Brooklyn. The same one, actually, but I work at night so much… " He gestured to the large windows. "Avoiding the light, you know? I put a bed and a couch here so I didn't have to wander home at three in the morning." He shrugged. "So, yeah, I suppose I live here."

He wandered over to set his keys in a beautiful ceramic bowl which was sitting on a table near a small kitchen area, and Kate jumped at the opportunity to look around at the walls of the studio which were littered with a personal tour of the mysterious Reed O'Connor's world.

A beautiful blue sari hung prominently on one wall; its silver thread caught the afternoon sun. She noticed a color picture of Dee hanging near it, captured in a group of laughing women. The woman at the center of the color photograph was elderly, and her laugh scribed deep recesses around her mouth as she looked into the camera. She was flanked by Dee on one side and a tall woman with blue eyes who appeared to be in her late fifties on the other. The blue-eyed woman wasn't laughing, but looked into the camera with a playful smile as her curly brown hair caught the sun.

As Kate strolled around the studio, she noticed his collection seemed to have no particular theme, though many of the styles were familiar. She recognized what could only have been one of Javi's abstract steel sculptures in one corner. The bright jewel-tones of Vanessa's art dotted the walls, along with various landscapes done mostly in acrylics. She did notice a few oil paintings scattered around the room, including a rustic cabin surrounded by pine trees, and another of a canopy of live oaks dripping with Spanish moss. She recognized a few of Dee's photographs hung along the walls, interspersed with some that appeared to be his own.

As she stood in front of the painting of the old cabin, she noticed the distinctive signature in the bottom right corner.

S. Rhodes.

"Sam Rhodes painted this?" She turned to look at the photographer, who had been watching her study the walls.

"Yeah, she sent that to me on my birthday one year. That's her grandfather's cabin. We used to go up there a lot. She lives there now. All her family lives in the mountains."

"Are any of the others her work?"

He nodded. "She'll send me one every now and then. Landscapes of California mostly. The beach, the Sierras. The Central Coast. Lots of places we visited together." He smiled a little. "I imagine she thinks it keeps me from getting homesick."

"Does it?"

He gave her a smile that didn't reach his eyes. "Not really."

A thousand questions flooded her mind as she continued walking around the room.

Kate stopped in front of one picture featuring a familiar square jaw. She smiled and turned to see him watching her with a curious expression.

She pointed at the picture. "This is Javi."

Reed raised an eyebrow at her, and his eyes seemed to light in amusement. "Yes, it is. He hates that picture. Ornery asshole tries to steal it on the rare occasions he ventures out of his cave and up in this direction."

The picture was taken from the front and showed the sculptor's mouth and jaw. His elaborate tattoos were visible along the collarbone, and she smiled when she saw the familiar flecked scars along his neck.

"Nice frame," she mused.

He walked toward her as she examined the picture. "Yeah, I like it." He lifted a hand over the picture, waving an index finger toward the sculptor's neck. "He's got some interesting scarring along his neck. You know, from the welding. Idiot used to forget to put his mask on. Good thing he's already so damn ugly," he said with a smile in her direction.

147

She felt her face flush and glanced away from the photographer's measuring gaze. She had forgotten for a moment that Javi and Reed were friends, and she wondered what Javi might have said about her, if anything.

Reed nodded toward another photograph mounted near Javi's portrait.

"That's Vanessa Allensworth."

Kate smiled, recognizing the regal profile. She was grateful for the change in subject. "Yeah, she says she loves that picture. She mentioned it when I met her."

He snorted. "I'm glad *she* likes it. Lydia hated it." He shrugged. "Of course, I didn't give a shit what Lydia thought. She's so damn bossy sometimes." He glanced at her out of the corner of his eye. "She's good, though. You're in good hands if you sign with her. She'll work her ass off for you."

They stood silently next to each other, unconsciously mirroring the other's stance as they looked at the various pieces of art that decorated the huge, white walls.

Kate caught a glint of silver from the corner of her eye as the light hit the sari again. She turned toward him and cocked her head. "Can I ask how you know Dee? She said it wasn't a secret or anything—it just wasn't her story to tell."

"Oh, sure." He walked toward the wall that held the sari. "No, it's not a secret. My mom was a hippie," he said with a small smile and an embarrassed shrug. "She was backpacking through India when she met my dad, who was some rich kid from Europe on holiday. They had a very short-lived affair, and she got knocked up."

Kate looked at him with a gaping mouth, and he chuckled ruefully. "Romantic, right? Anyway, he took off, and she didn't have enough money to get home, so she was stuck. Dee's grandmother, Dr. Mehra…" He nodded toward the photograph of the three women, "was the doctor at the clinic she went to, and she felt sorry for her. My mom didn't want to go back to the States, so she hired her to work in the house and stuff. So that's where I grew up. Dee and I were about the same age, so we played a lot, even though I was the neighborhood oddity. They're wonderful people, the Mehras. My mother became a nurse; she still takes care of Dr. Mehra. We moved to California with them when I was fifteen."

"That must have been an adjustment."

His laugh cracked the still air. "I was so relieved. Try to imagine being the tall American kid growing up in southern India." Kate laughed at the horrified expression on his face. "I always stood out like a sore thumb. *Hated* it. I still hate being the center of attention." He looked at the photograph again with a fond smile. "Dr. Mehra gave me my first camera when I was six. Wonderful woman."

He turned and walked toward the kitchen and Kate followed after him.

"Mr. O'Connor—"

"You can call me Reed," he said, smiling at her. "Mr. O'Connor seems a little formal at this point, Kate."

Kate stood speechless, suddenly realizing how awkward it was to stand in front of someone she had been studying for the past few months like a science experiment.

"Reed... I hope you aren't offended by what I said in Lydia's office. I don't know why I'm so curious about your life, I just am." She struggled to explain, "There's a portrait in the alumni gallery. Everyone calls it one of your early 'O'Connor portraits,' but it's not—not really. It's just a picture of a hand—*your* hand, I think— on a shoulder, and I've studied that picture for so many hours! Do you even remember the one I'm talking about?" She looked at him with pleading eyes.

A flash of raw pain crossed his face. "Yes," he said hoarsely. "Yes, I remember that one. I don't even know how the college got it."

"It's *different*, and it's always stuck with me," she said quietly. "I just—I guess it was always a mystery to me. Was that your hand? Who was the model? Was it her?" Kate held her breath. "Was it Sam?"

Reed trained his intense blue eyes on her. "You have a good eye. Javi was right. You have a good eye." He cleared his throat before he continued. "Yes, that portrait was special. And yes, that was my hand on Sam's shoulder."

Kate exhaled in relief, and a strange sort of satisfaction flooded her body, but tears came to her eyes as she looked at the dark-haired man standing in front of her, staring again at the painting of the solitary cabin. She had seen glimpses of the playful man Dee spoke of, and the moody artist Javi warned her about. She saw the lover that Vanessa had spoken of, but mostly, Kate saw a man in pain. Mustering her courage, she asked the question that had plagued her for months.

149

"Reed, what really happened to you and Sam?"

He stared at the painting for a few more moments before he glanced over at her and motioned toward the scarred wooden table in the kitchen area. He grabbed two bottles of water from the counter and handed one to her before he sat down. She followed him as he cracked it open, taking a long swallow before he cocked his head at her. She suddenly felt the strange focus so many others had talked about, trained intently on her, and she began to squirm.

Reed started speaking a couple of times, stopping each time before words could escape. She took a deep breath, forcing herself to be patient. Finally, he asked an unexpected question. "Do you dream a lot, Kate?"

"What?" She blinked. "Do I dream?" He nodded, so she continued, "Yeah, of course I dream. Maybe not every night, but fairly often."

He looked at her with haunted eyes and a wistful smile. "I dream. From the moment I met her, I have dreamt about Samantha Rhodes every night."

"What?"

Reed nodded slowly. "Every night. Weeks before I even kissed her, I dreamt that we were lovers. Then after we were, I would dream of us together like that, or just… anything, really. Talking. Joking. Working."

"That's…"

"Kind of different, I know."

"Yeah."

She sat across from him and took a sip of water as he stared at the table. "Do you still dream about her like that?"

"Yes."

"You dream about the woman you broke up with four years ago every night?"

A smile ghosted around his mouth.

She felt like she had to ask. "Reed, are you mentally ill?"

He laughed sharply and ran his fingers through his short hair, tugging it in a nervous gesture. "No, but I'm *really* irritable a lot of days."

"Yeah, no kidding."

He just chuckled and shook his head again. "Ask me if I mind."

Kate knew the answer, but asked anyway. "Do you mind dreaming about Sam every night?"

He shook his head, smiling sadly before he spoke again. "Samantha Rhodes"—He paused thoughtfully—"is the love of my life. My muse. My partner. She's necessary to me. Even if it's only in dreams. There was something about the way she made me look at the world and, maybe more important, *myself* that allowed me to focus all that energy I always felt buzzing around my brain. She... made the difference for me. The difference between being good and being great." He looked around the studio. "None of this would have been possible without her loving me."

Kate sat speechless, stunned silent by his words.

"And she did love me," Reed murmured. "And I loved her. Very much. I still love her. I'll always love her." He shrugged as if it was the most obvious thing in the world.

"Then why?" Kate shook her head. "Why aren't you together?"

He looked at her, the pain pouring out of his eyes. "Things happen, Kate. Mistakes get made... and bridges—even really strong ones—can burn."

He looked down at the table, tapping a finger thoughtfully and frowning at the dark wood grain.

"I imagine you found Brandon Wylie." His voice barely rose above a whisper. "Vanessa called and told me she gave you his name." He laughed bitterly. "I think she felt guilty, like she told you a secret or something."

"Yeah, I talked to him."

He nodded. "So you know. What I did, I mean. Which is fine. I don't mind you knowing, for some reason." He paused and rubbed his jaw nervously. "I messed up really bad, Kate; I hurt Sam at a time when she needed me—" He had to stop and clear his throat before he continued. "She needed me to be there for her, and I wasn't. How can I ask her to forgive me for something like that?" He shook his head, finally looking up at her. She thought she might have seen tears in his eyes.

"Have you asked her? To forgive you?"

Reed frowned and looked down at his hands, which were knit together in his lap. "I used to call her. Every day for a while, wanting to talk. To apologize. She never picked up the phone, so I finally started leaving these really long, rambling messages on her answering machine."

He paused before he continued quietly. "I told her I was sorry. I told her about... about what I was doing, or people we knew here. Stuff I saw in the city. I was still trying to be sort of social at that point. For her. She always said I'd be a hermit if she didn't drag me out of the studio." He smiled. "She was right, I guess."

"That you became a hermit?"

Reed shrugged. "Yes. Aren't I?"

He looked down at his hands again, twisting them nervously. "I got frustrated eventually, maybe six months or so after she left?" He looked up and out the bright windows.

"I was angry that she wouldn't talk to me. Angry that she seemed willing to throw away what we had, everything we'd been through. And, I have a pretty bad temper sometimes. We both do," he muttered under his breath. "And we can both be really stubborn. She still never called me back, no matter what I said. I guess I wasn't expecting her to at that point."

Kate saw him shake his head, but he continued speaking in a low voice.

"I started dating random people. Stupid girls who thought I was glamorous or some shit like that. I think I was hoping she'd have a reaction, get pissed off or something. She never did. Javi did! He got so pissed, he didn't talk to me for about eight months, but Sam…"

Reed pointed toward the painting of the cabin on the lake. "She sent that to me for my birthday that spring. I didn't call her again after that. I knew she wasn't coming back at that point. I still checked in with Susan for a while, just to make sure she was okay, but I figured—I figure she wanted to move on with her life."

"Why… I mean, do you know why—"

"There were just too many memories here, I think." He took a deep breath. "Too much history. But she still sends me a painting every now and then. I like getting them."

"The landscapes?" Kate asked.

He nodded. "She used to paint *me*, you know? She had so many canvases of me." He smiled. "I used to pretend it bugged me sometimes, sitting for her, but really I loved it. I loved to see her put all that focus on me. She's so talented. She only paints landscapes now. Beautiful stuff. Just gorgeous. I mean, her use of light—" Reed stopped himself, shaking his head and smiling a little. "Yeah, not really what we were talking about…"

Kate smiled at his enthusiasm over his former lover's work.

"Anyway," he continued, "her portrait work was even better than her landscapes. The way she would capture the subtlety of expression on a subject's face. Her work was stunning. She was extraordinary. She still is." He looked into the distance, staring out the windows of the studio again.

"I've never seen any of her portrait work," Kate offered. "I saw some sketches she did, though. They're hanging up in the alumni gallery now. Just anatomy studies… but they're really good," she added quickly.

"They're probably of me."   He smiled slowly. "Anatomy, huh?"

Kate rolled her eyes. "Not *that* kind of anatomy!"

Reed chuckled. "Well, she did a lot of those too, you know."

"Such a guy."

He continued to laugh and crossed his arms over his chest. "So prudish, Kate.   Haven't you ever wanted to take pictures of someone? Pictures of *everything*?" He cocked an eyebrow at her, and his smile was devilish. "That's half the fun of being an artist, you know?   You get to call naked pictures 'nudes' and act intellectual about them."

"You know, it's always the good-looking male photographers who have girls falling all over them. They're the ones who do the nudes."

"I never claimed different," he said. "Oh, wait… I know what you should do."

"Oh yeah? Enlighten me, genius."

"A series on tattoos. I heard you might be inspired."

Reed grinned at her blush, but Kate just shook her head and flipped him off as he laughed harder. Slowly, the tension drained out of the room and before she knew it, they were both laughing.

They started trading stories about the more pretentious aspects of the art world. Reed told Kate about what portraits he was working on, and he asked her in detail about the self-portrait series she was shooting in Javi's warehouse.

"You're brave," Reed admitted. "Braver than me. I've never had the guts to put myself in front of the camera."

She shrugged. "I don't really feel all that brave. It's just necessary for me. At least it is right now. I'm happy with how they're turning out. And I'm *so* grateful that Javi is letting me use his studio."

"Oh yeah?"

"Yeah, I mean—" Kate couldn't help the blush that colored her face again when she thought about the sculptor. "I know he's really private. I was surprised he let me in his studio at all, much less to take pictures there. I never thought he'd say yes when I asked."

Reed raised an inquisitive eyebrow. "I'm not going to lie, it's unusual for him. He must think a lot of you." A small smile flickered around his mouth.

Her blush only grew. "That's good to hear. I mean, he's a great artist. His vision for his work, and then his craftsmanship, too. So, you know, it's gratifying to hear he thinks so much of *my* work. And he recommended me to Lydia, I guess, which is just —" She shook her head. "Amazing, you know?"

Reed let her ramble, a smile continuing to ghost around his lips. "Javi's one of my best friends. Probably my best friend, other than Sam."

"Yeah?"

He nodded and leaned forward over the table. "So, Kate, I have to tell you—and you can take this however you like—I've *never* seen Javi share his space with anyone before. Not me. Not Vanessa. No one."

Kate's heart raced. "No one?"

"Never."

Reed leaned back in his chair, a slight smile still dancing on his lips. He watched her silently, and she tried to get her blush under control, but she couldn't help but think about Javi's brusque demeanor around the warehouse, and the heat she sensed in his eyes when she caught him watching her.

"He thinks I'm a kid," Kate said quietly.

Reed frowned. "Do you think he'd let a kid use his workspace? Do you think he'd respect a kid enough for that?"

Her mind raced with the possibilities of what he was saying, but she couldn't quite wrap her brain around the implications. She cleared her throat and tried to play it off. "Oh, he might share his studio with a kid, if the kid could fetch beer, cigarettes, and tacos fast enough."

Reed's face split into a grin before he burst into laughter.

"Kate," he finally said, still laughing a little. "I'm really glad I met you."

"Me, too."

She liked him. Once you got past the sadness that seemed to hang around his tall shoulders, Reed O'Connor exhibited a great sense of humor, a fierce passion about his art, and an obvious affection and loyalty for his friends.

"Why does everyone say you're such an asshole?" she finally asked after another round of crazy photo shoot stories. "Brandon Wylie talks about you like you're a total creep."

He snorted. "Wylie... I'd like to think that's more a reflection on him than me. Though admittedly, I wasn't very nice to him. The asshole part? I've been told that I'm very... focused when I'm working; I'm sure I'm getting worse in my old age." He smirked a little. "Plus, I'm loaded now, which means I can tell everyone to fuck off if they don't like my stuff."

He shrugged again. "I think celebrities think too much of themselves. I enjoy examining them. Sometimes, they really *are* quite beautiful, but often, their beauty is so fake. Like a thin layer of snow over a dirty street. I have no interest in taking a picture of the same nose sculpted by the same surgeon on five different actresses. It's boring and more than a little insulting, if you think about it. Like they know better than we do what beauty is."

"I'd never thought about it like that before."

From there, Kate and Reed launched into a discussion of his work and how it related to her thesis project. He agreed to allow her to use some quotes in her published thesis, for which she was flattered and very grateful.

"Reed." Kate paused, finally getting up the courage to ask what had been on her mind for hours. "Do you still have any pictures of Sam?"

He smiled. "Of course. Would you like to see some?"

"Very much."

Reed stood and motioned her toward the walled-off area of the studio. Turning the corner, she saw a small living area containing a couch, a neatly made bed pushed into a corner, and bookcases which lined two of the walls. On the other two walls were picture after picture of Samantha Rhodes.

Some were art pieces, dramatically lit and processed, featuring O'Connor's distinctive abstract style. They were stunning, and Kate recognized a few of them she had seen in exhibits and others that had been published. The rest were candid shots—all showing Sam's face—where the blond woman was laughing, working, or often just looking into the camera with a soft smile and a warm look in her brown eyes. There were color prints and black and whites, and all of them captured her beauty in different ways.

Kate noticed an abstract canvas highlighted in the center of one wall. Upon closer inspection, she realized that it wasn't abstract, just unfinished. She stared at it, finally recognizing the familiar lines and angles of the picture Dee had taken of them in college. Sam must have started it, but left it unfinished for some reason.

"Do you still have the picture? The one Dee took?" Kate asked softly, as she went to stand in front of the unfinished canvas.

Reed stood next to her, his right hand gripping his short hair, and the other hanging limply at his side as he stared at the unfinished oil painting.

"No," he whispered. "I was so stupid. After the fight—after she left and she ripped up all her canvases, I lost it. I tore up all the prints I had of her. I tore up *that* picture without thinking." He sighed deeply as he looked at the painting. "So stupid. I could reprint all the ones I had taken, but I didn't have the negative for that one."

"Why didn't you ask Dee for another copy?"

"I didn't really deserve another copy, did I? This is all I have left. It's not complete, but I love it."

Kate looked at him and tears threatened her eyes when she saw the sadness and resignation on Reed's face. She reached over and took his hand, squeezing his fingers in her own, and she felt him squeeze back lightly.

"Do you think she still has hers?" she asked.

He stared at the unfinished oil.

"Maybe." He paused. "I hope so. Maybe if she did…"

Kate looked at him out of the corner of her eye as he trailed off.

"Yeah…" she murmured. "Maybe."

CHAPTER TWENTY-FOUR

Crestline, California
July 2007

"You should call him."

"What would I say after a year, Suz? What could I possibly say to make things right again?"

Susan scowled at Sam as they sat on the front porch of their grandfather's cabin on the lake, watching the sun set over the mountains. An owl hooted in the pine trees surrounding them, and she could hear trout jumping in the twilight.

"Say you're better! Say that the idiot doctors should have warned you about depression when you lost the baby. Say that you want to come home." Susan grabbed her cousin's hand and whispered desperately. "Say you forgive him, Sammy. Say you love him. I *know* you still do."

Sam dashed the tears from her eyes and pulled her hand away. "I forgive *him*?" she hissed. "I'm the one who was so messed up. *I'm* the one who flipped out when I knew how stressed out he was. He'd been holding me together for so long..." she whispered, shaking her head. "I saw the look on his face as soon as he kissed that stupid girl, and I completely lost it instead of talking to him like a rational person. All—*all* my canvases—" She choked, and the tears ran down her face.

After Sam had shown up at Susan's the previous summer, her cousin finally grilled her about how she'd been coping. Sam knew her work had dropped off. That she was sleeping more than normal and dropping weight, but she was just never hungry. She'd had no perspective from the dark hole she found herself in. Susan, who had grown up with a mother who battled clinical depression, recognized the symptoms almost immediately.

'Sam, it's me. Will you please talk to me? I don't understand. Why are you doing this? Aren't you even willing to listen to me? I don't want to apologize to a machine.'

After a difficult conversation with a lot of yelling on Susan's part, which was mostly met by detached numbness on Sam's, she had agreed to go to a doctor in Southern California. Together, they began to get a handle on the illness that should have been dealt with months before.

'Please, pick up the phone, baby. We need to work this out. We can work this out, Sammy. Just… pick up the phone. Please.'

Though she'd been getting better and her doctor was pleased with her progress, Sam still refused to even talk with Reed on the phone when he called. She knew the things she'd said had been unforgivable, and she was worried what else she might say if she got too upset.

Reed had called the house daily for weeks, finally leaving lengthy phone messages when she refused to answer. At first they were heart-rending, then they were resigned. Finally, after months of Sam ignoring him, Reed became angry.

'That's it, huh? Six years, but you're willing to just throw it away like this? You're so fucking stubborn. Why am I even bothering to call anymore? Why don't you tell me? Tell me, Samantha!'

Sam knew he still called Susan occasionally to make sure she was okay, but she'd forbidden Susan from revealing how bad the depression had been. Eventually, the phone calls had petered off, and Susan heard from Lydia that Reed had been seeing other people.

She told herself that it was good.

"Sammy, you *weren't* a rational person. You were clinically depressed. You need to tell him that. He's never known the whole story, and it's not fair. He needs to hear it from *you*. Don't you think he would want to know?"

Sam dashed the tears from her eyes. "You don't get it, Susan. You weren't there. I said such horrible things. Awful things. Things I knew weren't true. And I said them anyway. You can't unsay things like that."

"Please talk to him; you know he would understand."

Sam shook her head. All she could hear was Reed pleading for forgiveness as she ripped her canvases apart. Then the crash of the light kits and the eerie silence that followed.

"I told him I didn't need him," she whispered. "That he could never give me what I needed, and that he was holding me back." She choked on her tears as she continued. "I told him it was a good thing I lost the baby, because he was too self-centered to be a father."

She heard Susan gasp as the tears rolled down her face. "Sammy—"

"How on earth could he still love someone who would say that to him? How could he even look at me again?" Sam stood, pacing back and forth on the porch as she stared at the full moon rising over the mountains. "He deserves to be with someone who would never say something like that."

Sam turned to her cousin with pleading eyes. "I *know* he still feels guilty, but that will pass, and he'll find someone who's *good* for him. Who's healthy and whole. Didn't Javi tell Vanessa he was seeing that performance artist?"

Susan snorted. "Yeah, she also said she had to restrain Javi from flying up to New York so he didn't kick the shit out of Reed."

"That's not fair," she whispered. "He deserves to be happy." She nodded. "He'll find someone to make him happy."

"*You* make him happy."

She shook her head. "No, I don't. I hadn't made him happy in months."

"That's not true. You loved him. Even when you were sick, you loved him, and he knew that." Susan came to stand behind her and put her arms around Sam's waist. She had lost so much weight, she almost felt like Susan could snap her in two.

Her cousin leaned her chin on Sam's shoulder as they looked out at the dark lake. The stars reflected off the cold water, and it reminded Sam of the lake in the middle of Central Park where Reed liked to take pictures. He had sent her one the previous month. It was just a snapshot, but Sam had taped it to the fridge along with all the other random pictures of the city Reed kept sending.

"Don't you love him anymore?"

"Of course I love him." Sam shrugged like it was the most obvious thing in the world. "I'll *always* love him."

"So why—"

"He deserves better than this mess."

CHAPTER TWENTY-FIVE

Pomona, California
July 2010

Kate let herself into the warehouse late on Thursday night with the key Javi had given her, quietly picking her way through the studio toward the small office in back. None of the lights were on, and she didn't hear music blasting, so she guessed he had gone home for the night.

She'd driven directly from the airport, thankful that she had been able to sleep on Susan's plush private jet. She was on her way home when she remembered one of her lenses was still in Pomona, and she needed it the next morning.

Kate wasn't tired, despite the time change, and she hummed happily as she maneuvered through the scrap metal that littered the floor. She smiled at the thin path Javi always seemed to clear for her leading toward the back office. She wondered if he even realized he did it.

She couldn't stop thinking about what Reed said about him. Was she really the only other artist he had ever let use his studio? She knew she was fascinated by him. Did he really see her as more than a kid he was helping out as a favor to Dee?

Kate picked up a worn work shirt that had fallen to the ground and draped it over the back of a chair. Javi often stripped down to just an undershirt after he finished working, sweat pouring off of his arms and back from the heat of the torch and the weight of his leather sleeves. She flashed to the memory of him the week before, standing over the beginnings of a new piece wearing only a pair of jeans, his cow hide chaps and a sweat-soaked t-shirt. The sculptor had caught her eyes and stared at her. Kate had to fight the urge to grab her camera.

No man had ever affected her the way Javi did. She was past trying to deny it or try to reason through it. He had become her fascination. He may not have been classically handsome, but something about the rough sculptor drew her in.

"Like a moth to a flame." She sighed as she pried open the door.

Kate turned the lights on in the office and was looking through her bag of lenses when the door slammed open. She gasped as she stepped back, and her foot twisted in the leg of the chair behind her, causing her to stumble and fall. She landed with a small 'oomph' as Javi strode into the room.

"Shit, Katie! What the hell are you doing here? I thought someone was robbing the place!" He blinked at her in confusion and tossed aside the length of steel pipe he'd been holding.

She scowled as she rubbed her forehead where she'd bumped it on the desk. "I was just getting a lens! I didn't think you were even here. All the lights were off."

He knelt beside her and pushed her hair back to look at her forehead. "I was working late," he said in a gravelly voice. "I crashed on that bed I have in the back. Did you hit anything else or just your forehead? Let me see. It's not bleeding, but you'll have a bump."

Javi pushed the chair back and disentangled her ankle with gentle hands. He was bare from the waist up, and Kate's eyes were drawn to the defined muscles at his waist and abdomen.

"N—no," she stuttered as she took in his brightly painted chest. "I'm fine." Most of his tattoos were flames. She had examined the blue and green patterns on his arms and shoulders, but had never seen the bright red and gold fire that licked up his torso and spread over his chest. She couldn't stop staring.

"You sure you're okay?" He frowned at her blank expression, and the color rushed to her face. He glanced down at his naked chest, as if just realizing he was only half-dressed. "Oh, sorry. I'll, uh… I'll go put a shirt on. I was sleeping."

"It's okay. I'm not—I mean… they're beautiful." She blushed even brighter when she realized he had caught her staring at his chest. "Your tattoos. I've never seen all of them. They're... beautiful."

He was still holding on to her ankle, and she felt his thumb brush along the curve of her calf. He looked down, his sleepy eyes tracing along her legs as he knelt between them. Her heart began to race, and she leaned forward. Javi quickly rocked back on his heels and stood, silently holding out a hand to help her to her feet.

"How was New York?"

She tried to ignore the rush of disappointment as he distanced himself. She grasped his hand and stood. "Good. It was good." Kate turned back to the desk to zip up her lens case.

"Reed said he enjoyed meeting you, which is unusual for him."

She smiled, knowing he didn't intend it as an insult.

"He called you?" She swung around to catch him staring at her legs with hooded eyes. Javi blinked again and cleared his throat.

"Yeah. Yeah, we talked this afternoon."

"What did he say?"

He stared at her, and Kate wondered if he would even answer.

"He said I was lucky." His eyes raced over her face, lingering a little on her slightly parted mouth. "To be working with you, I mean. He thinks you're really talented."

"Oh." She nodded and forced a smile. "That's really flattering."

"Yeah."

They stood across from each other, both silent as tension blanketed the room. Her heart was racing. She couldn't tear her eyes away from the swirling flames that covered him. She wanted to trace each curling flame with her fingers. Was his skin as smooth as it looked? Or would it be rough? His hands would be rough. But strong. Kate saw an anvil marking the inside of his bicep.

She wanted to sink her teeth into it.

Kate finally lifted her eyes to meet Javi's. Her knees almost gave out when she saw the unguarded hunger in his sleepy stare. Her heart sped up, and she took a tentative step toward him. Reed's words rushed back to her.

"I've never seen Javi share his space with anyone before."
"No one?"
"Never."

Taking a deep breath, Kate took another step toward him, only to see Javi step back from her and cross his arms over his chest. He frowned and looked at her feet. It didn't matter anymore. She had seen the invitation in his eyes.

"Did you twist your ankle or anything?"

"Javi—"

"You should probably get some sleep. I'm sure you're exhausted."

"I slept on the plane."

He stood motionless, like one of the statues he created, his arms crossed and his shoulders tense. Kate stepped toward him again, but this time, Javi didn't move away. Her heart was pounding when she lifted a hand to his bare chest. He sucked in a breath as she ran a tentative finger along one of the flames that started over his heart, tracking it up his chest, until her finger lay over his collarbone.

She felt his massive body shiver under her touch as he exhaled a rough breath. Looking up to meet his dark eyes, she stood on her tiptoes and leaned forward until her lips met his. Kate held them to his for a moment, waiting... hoping he would kiss her back. Finally, she felt Javi's surprisingly soft lips move a fraction as a rough sound escaped his throat.

Kate drew back, unsure of his reaction. His shoulders were still tense and his arms remained crossed, but his mouth gaped a little, as if in shock. Her face flaming, she stepped away from him, turning toward the desk to grab her bag so she could make a quick exit.

"Kate."

Plastering on a blank expression, she turned. Javi stepped toward her, reached a rough hand out to cup the back of her neck, and pulled her into his arms. His lips crashed into hers and his left arm came around to grip her waist and weld her against his body. She felt his fingers thread through the hair at the nape of her neck as he tilted her head to angle her mouth toward his. Hard lips devoured hers and when she gasped, Javi only pulled her closer. Her head swam and Kate lifted her arms around his neck; a soft whimper escaped her throat.

He drew back immediately. "Am I hurting—"

Javi couldn't finish his question, because Kate pulled him back and kissed him again. She pressed her body to his, reveling in the heat of his arms. The strength. She dug her fingers into his shoulders. His upper body was hard as stone from years of working with metal and concrete, but his callused hand stroked her neck gently as he kissed her with the same intensity and focus he had when he held a torch.

Yes, she thought. *More*. This was what she needed.

He finally pulled away from her. "Kate," he panted. "I don't —" He cleared his throat, still eyeing her lips as his fingers flexed at the small of her back. "What the hell are we doing?"

She took one hand from his neck and ran it along his jaw until her fingertips traced his lips. "Kissing." She leaned in and softly bit over the spark scars along his neck.

He let out a low growl and pulled her lips back to his. "You know what I mean," he mumbled against her mouth. Javi's arms were tightly controlled power, but his lips... his lips were soft and hungry.

"I really don't," she said.

"Is this—" He broke away and tilted her chin up to press kisses along the soft skin of her neck. "Are you going through some..." Kate's eyes rolled back when she felt the soft tug of his fingers twisting in her hair. "...some bad-boy, ugly-artist phase?"

"You're most definitely not a boy. And there's nothing ugly about you, Javi," she whispered.

He drew back and met her eyes. The overwhelming hunger she had seen earlier had softened. The tension left his shoulders, and his hands relaxed against her skin. He pressed a single, soft kiss to her mouth as his fingers explored the curves of her face.

"Why me?"

She smiled. "Because you see me, and I see you. And because..." Kate reached up and pressed her cheek to his as she whispered in his ear, "You're more than you think you are."

He reached up and cupped her face, looking directly into her eyes when he spoke. "If we do this, it's gonna be real. You and me. Meet the family. All that stuff. I'm too old to play around with this shit."

"You know, Javi, I don't think anyone would take you for a casual kind of guy. Especially not me."

He smirked, and his thumbs brushed against the soft skin of her jaw. "So no fooling around?"

Her eyebrows lifted. "Well, I don't know about *that*."

Kate was surprised to see the bashful smile cross his lips. "I didn't mean... that. Exactly."

She smiled a little. "Good, because I like some kinds of fooling around."

"I just mean…" He frowned and placed a hand over her heart. "I want something real with you, Katie. With us. I'm not a kid, so if that's not what you're looking for—"

"It is. That's what I want, too. Something real. And something honest."

Javi's smile dropped, and he looked her dead in the eye. "I will *never* lie to you."

Kate snorted a little. "Oh, I know you won't. Even the few times I might *want* you to, I'm sure you'll be brutally honest."

He shrugged and put an arm around her, tugging her toward the door leading out to the warehouse. "I might learn to be… slightly less brutal," he muttered as he shut off the lights and led her toward the kitchen.

"Just be you." She leaned over and touched her lips to his shoulder, smiling against his skin. "I've become surprisingly attached to that guy."

Javi stopped and drew her into another kiss. Kate was overwhelmed by how gently he held her. Like she was glass. Something precious and delicate. And she remembered the hands that swung a hammer could also set a tiny stone.

He pulled away. "I never expected this. I wasn't looking for you."

"I guess that's what you get for letting me into the warehouse."

His face broke into a rare and brilliant smile as he pushed her in front of him to walk the labyrinth of scrap metal. His hands stayed at her waist and she placed her own on top of his, threading their fingers together.

"What am I going to do with you?"

"I have some ideas. A few of them. You could say this place has inspired me."

Kate heard his low chuckle. "None of that, at least not tonight. I need to, you know, take you out and shit. And take a shower. I probably stink."

She leaned back into his chest. "You smell fine. And you're going to take me out?"

"Of course I'm going to take you out. That's what you do."

"We going out for something other than tacos?"

He paused. "Maybe."

She turned and grinned at him, realizing she had unwittingly become an expert at reading the taciturn man in the weeks they had spent together. His mouth may have been twisted in a slight scowl, but his eyes were warm and happy. They were also tinged with exhaustion, and she wondered how many days he had been working.

"Javi?" She turned toward him, his hands still clinging to her waist.

"Hmm?"

"I don't want to leave. Do you mind if I stay? Just to sleep?"

A low growl came from his throat, but he nodded, pulling her toward the low bed tucked into the corner of the warehouse behind a makeshift screen. She toed off her shoes, and Javi pulled her down, tucking her in front of him as he lay on his side. He kissed her temple once before he fell back in exhaustion. Then, he draped an arm across her waist and released a deep sigh when she pressed her back into his chest.

Kate smiled, thinking that they fit together like mismatched puzzle pieces. Her fingers tracked up and down his forearm, softly tracing the outline of the green flame that covered it. After a few minutes, she felt him relax behind her.

"Katie?"

"Yeah?"

He leaned forward, barely whispering in a sleepy voice. "I missed you."

Her heart swelled as she nestled into the warm comfort of his embrace. Javi's breathing evened out, and she smiled into the darkness and closed her eyes.

"I missed you, too."

Part Ten: The Muse

CHAPTER TWENTY-SIX

Crestline, California
August 2010

A soft, dry dust kicked up from Kate's wheels as she turned into the small clearing in front of the log cabin at the edge of the lake. Dee had given her directions to Sam Rhodes's home in the mountains, but not her phone number, so Kate wasn't sure whether the painter would even be there, though Dee assured her that Sam was usually there and working during the week.

Kate was relieved to see the lone figure on the dock standing next to an easel. She parked the car, got out, and resisted the urge to grab her camera and capture the scene.

The light was perfect, and the midmorning sun captured the gold highlights of the woman's dark blond hair. She stood leaning on one foot while her right arm worked; her head was cocked, studying the scene she was painting.

A small wooden boat was tied to the end of the dock, and it rocked slowly in the quiet water. Kate could hear the small waves slap against the wooden pilings as she walked toward the woman she'd heard about for months.

She was halfway down before she heard her call out.

"Stay back there!"

She didn't turn around, but her voice carried in the still morning air.

"I'll talk to you in a few minutes, but I'm right in the middle of this."

Kate hesitated, looking at the woman, and then back to her car.

"Should I go? I can wait in my car if you want."

"No. I'll ignore you. Just sit down there and don't get in my light."

Kate sat on the edge of the dock, kicking her legs over the edge, and staring into the blue water of the lake high in the San Bernardino Mountains. After another half an hour, she heard the woman at the end of the dock begin to move around. Kate stood, brushed off her legs, and approached cautiously.

"Can I help?"

The painter finally turned and looked at her, and Kate got her first look at Reed O'Connor's muse.

She was smiling, and her eyes squinted a little in the bright sun. She was older than the woman in the photographs, and faint lines marked the corners of her mouth. Her hair was a little shorter and swept her shoulders, but her brown eyes were familiar, warm, and friendly. She wore a simple pair of blue jeans, a stained green t-shirt, and her feet were bare.

"You must be Kaitlyn." She wiped her hands on a rag, but didn't offer to shake.

"I am. It's just Kate, though."

She kept wiping her hands. "Nice to meet you, Kate."

"You're Samantha Rhodes."

Suddenly, the painter smiled, and it transformed her pretty face into something infinitely more beautiful.

"Yep, I'm Samantha Rhodes."

And just as suddenly, Kate understood why the painter's face had haunted Reed's dreams for so many years. None of her features were particularly eye-catching in isolation, but taken all together, Sam was a stunning woman. Her eyes brimmed with life, and the air around her almost seemed to vibrate. She turned back to the easel and started packing up the paints she'd been using. Kate stepped forward.

"Can I call you Sam?"

"That's fine."

Sam continued to pack up her things, and Kate saw her take a deep breath before she spoke again.

"You know, my ears have been burning for about five months now." The tubes of paint went into a box. "I hear you ask good questions." She looked over her shoulder, and Kate caught a twinkle in her eye.

The younger woman shrugged and let her hands hang in her pockets, unsure of what she could do to help. Sam handed Kate a box of paints and an unfinished canvas to hold as she folded up the easel and tucked it under her arm. She quickly wrapped her brushes and palette, then traded them for the canvas and started walking back toward shore, allowing Kate to follow with the rest.

Kate fumbled the box and brushes as she walked, wondering how the artist did this without an extra arm. "I didn't mean to interrupt."

Sam kept walking, pausing to slip on a pair of flip-flops at the edge of the clearing. "The light was changing. There's only a window, you know? I'll come back tomorrow. It'll be here."

Kate followed after her, walking over the gravel driveway toward the painter's home, still carrying the case of paints she'd handed her. Sam walked up to the old cabin, placed the easel on a paint-smudged table on the porch, and opened the screen door, holding it for Kate to walk inside.

"Let me go put this upstairs," Sam said as she started up the stairs at the back of the living room. "Take my stuff to the kitchen. I'll be right back."

Kate nodded and stood in the small living area, examining the rugged stone fireplace and log walls which were decorated with art. It was old, but clean and uncluttered except for the art.

Paintings and photographs lined the room, and surfaces sported small sculptures, ceramic pieces, and blown glass work. Kate saw some of Vanessa's canvases hanging next to a portrait of Chris and Dee's daughter. A delicately worked wrought-iron mirror that looked like Javi's work hung over the fireplace, and a ruby red vase adorned the mantle.

"You have a lot of art," Kate murmured.

"I know a lot of artists," Sam said as she walked down the stairs.

Kate followed as Sam walked down a dark hall toward a kitchen with large windows and mid-century appliances.

"So, I imagine you want to talk about Reed," Sam said nonchalantly.

"Kind of." Kate was still looking around.

"Well, that's an unusual answer." Sam paused and cocked her head toward Kate. "Give me one good reason I should talk to you about him."

She paused. The painter didn't look unfriendly, just cautious. But behind the caution, Kate could also sense the low burn of curiosity flickering in Sam's eyes.

"I want to understand him. I want to understand his work, and why it's so important. To me. To your friends. To everyone, I guess."

Sam shrugged. "So why talk to me?"

"Someone told me once that if I wanted to understand Reed O'Connor, I had to understand Samantha Rhodes."

A slow smile grew on Sam's face and she nodded toward a small kitchen table where Kate sat down. Sam reached over to grab the brushes and palette and take them to the counter.

"That was Chris wasn't it? Who said that?" Sam chuckled as she began to rinse out her brushes. "Yeah, that was Chris."

"It was sort of a Jedi Master moment for him."

Sam looked over her shoulder with a smile before breaking into a bold laugh. "Oh, Kate," she said. "I think I'm going to like you. Want some water?"

"Sure." Kate looked around the room. "I like your house." The kitchen looked like it hadn't been changed since the 1960s, and cheerful gingham curtains hung over large windows that looked over the lake. She couldn't help but notice the scattering of black and white photographs that covered the old refrigerator. They looked like cityscapes of New York.

"Thanks. I like it too. When things aren't broken, that is. I grew up here—not in this house, but I spent a lot of time here. It used to be my grandfather's."

"He passed away?"

"Yeah, but I keep expecting him to come out of the studio or walk through the front door after a morning of fishing."

"How long ago?"

She frowned a little. "I guess... six—no seven years ago. Yeah, seven. He gave me and Susan the cabin. It was always our favorite place. Susan lives across the lake with her husband now, so the cabin's mine."

"There's a studio? Upstairs?"

"Yep. My grandfather was a painter; he's the first person that ever gave me a paint brush. I spent most of my childhood copying him. Sometimes on his canvases, sometimes on the walls."

She was patting her brushes with paper towel and putting them in old mason jars when she nodded toward the wall near the table.

Kate leaned closer to see the small childish outline of a green duck painted on the log.

Kate smiled. "Did he yell at you?"

"Oh, no." Sam shook her head as she filled two more jars with ice water. "He just laughed." She walked across the kitchen, sitting across from Kate and handing her the jar of water. Sam leaned forward and clinked the edges together.

"Nice to finally meet you, Kate Mitchell. Here's to telling stories."

"Here's to listening."

Sam smiled and leaned her elbows on the table; Kate noticed the brown paint that freckled her forearms. "I do like you. I see why Dee does, too. I think... you're like Reed, aren't you? You see things."

"I hope so. I try to."

"I hear you've talked to everyone now. You even got an audience with the man."

Kate snorted. "Is that how everyone thinks of him?"

Sam smiled and shrugged. "People tend to revolve around him. They're attracted to his talent, his vision. He's magnetic. The way he sees the world, it's just not like anyone else, you know? So people tend to circle in varying degrees of orbit."

She paused to take a drink. "To be honest, it always sort of freaked him out. He doesn't really like most people. He hates being the center of attention."

"So, people revolved around him, but he revolved around you?"

Sam raised an eyebrow as she looked at Kate. "Don't kid yourself. I was as much in his orbit as anyone." She paused for a moment, tracking a drip of water that fell down the side of her jar. "I suppose—if we're being fair—we orbited around each other. And when we did..."

"It was extraordinary."

"Yes." She nodded. "It was extraordinary."

Kate frowned a little. "I'm still not sure I get what everyone means by that."

Sam paused for a moment. "I'm very talented, Kate. I do great work. But I think I was only *really* talented when we were together."

"Why?"

Sam shrugged. "What explanation is there for chemistry? We just worked. We focused each other." She paused again. "It was like Reed—when he was 'on'—could relax me and excite me all at the same time. And hopefully I did the same thing for him. I think I did, except toward the end. Then I was just so messed up."

"Can you... would you tell me what got messed up?"

Sam looked down at the table and drew her finger through a water spot before she answered in a quiet voice. "I, um... I was depressed." She looked up to meet Kate's eyes. "Not moody-artistic-temperament-depressed, but actually *clinically* depressed, and we didn't see it. I didn't see it." She smiled wistfully. "We were so young. Not much older than you, and we had no idea. You get down in that pit and you don't really know how to get out. And you think you should be able to fix it, but you're not even sure what's wrong to begin with. It wasn't until I got back here and got some help that I started to get better." She looked out the windows which glittered in the midday sun. "It took a long time to get better," she whispered.

Kate stared at her, still haunted by so many questions.

"But you did? Get better, I mean."

Sam nodded. "Yeah, I did." She took a deep breath and smiled again. "And I've built a good life here. It's not the life I expected when I was younger, but it's good. I love the work I'm doing now, and I love the mountains. Plus," she said with a grin, "Lydia can't harp on me when I'm out in the middle of nowhere, can she?"

Kate smiled. "Does she still represent you?"

"Sort of." Sam shrugged. "As much as anyone does. Most of my work is commission now, so I don't do the gallery shows and exhibitions that I used to. I like it, though. I'm not rich, but I have enough. And it lets me live where I want to."

Kate looked out the windows at the isolated mountain lake. "What do you do up here?"

Sam cocked an eyebrow at the young woman. "Well, Kate, I live my life."

She stammered a little, blushing. "I—I didn't mean—"

"It's okay," Sam said. "You carry yourself with so much confidence, it's easy to forget how young you are. I felt the same way when I was your age, very eager to get away. To go to school and immerse myself in art. I was very focused. Very driven."

"But you came back?"

"Yes, I did. The older I get, the more I realize how much of life doesn't happen in the very small bubble of the artistic community. And that's what we're trying to paint, isn't it? Life? Hope, fear, love, doubt?"

"And you found that here?"

"It's all tied together, Kate. And you don't need to be in New York or Los Angeles or San Francisco to see it. It's good to remember that." She took a long swallow of water and looked out the window. "I like going to church with my aunt occasionally or painting a landscape to donate to a local charity or old-folks home. I like looking where I played as a child with older, and hopefully wiser, eyes. There's more depth here than I ever recognized when I was young."

"You didn't like New York?"

Sam's eyebrows shot up. "I loved New York! I was so excited to go. I loved my time there. What this place is for landscape and light, New York is for people. The variety, the energy—it's intoxicating. And the sheer amount of talent it draws is astounding. No." She shook her head. "Don't get me wrong. I loved living in New York."

"Why didn't you ever go back?"

Sam paused for a moment. "New York is Reed," she said. "And Reed has moved on. Which is for the best."

Kate's mouth fell open. "Why do you say that?"

"A lot of reasons," she said.

The haunted expression Kate had seen on Reed's face settled over Sam's.

Kate leaned forward on the table, frowning. "Please help me understand what happened. I know it's not any of my business, I know I'm being completely nosy, but I feel like I need to understand."

Sam looked at her, all expression carefully wiped away. "But why?"

Kate paused, staring at the table and thinking of her growing feelings for Javi. What she felt for him was so much bigger than anything she'd felt for anyone before and sometimes, it scared her. "You and Reed... you loved each other so much. You had something that everyone looks for and so few people find. And it seems like you two lost it... threw it away. How could you—"

"We didn't 'throw it away!'"

"Then what happened? Really?"

Sam clenched her eyes together and took a deep breath. "We need..."

Kate leaned forward. "What?"

"Wine," she said, scooting back from the table and plastering on a smile.

"Wine?"

"Yes, wine. I know it's not even noon, but I think this conversation needs wine. Grab a couple of glasses from that cabinet to the left of the sink. I'll get a bottle from the pantry."

"Okay." Kate was confused, but she nodded and stood up, walking to the cabinet Sam had pointed toward. As she opened the cupboard, she noticed a flash of color on the inside of the door. She looked to her left and her mouth dropped open when she saw what it was.

Taped on the inside of the cabinet was the old photograph of Reed and Sam she had seen in Dee's studio months ago. The print looked as if it had been pulled off and stuck down many times, and she could see fingerprints smudged along the edges. Kate stared at it, gently touching a corner curled by age.

"Please don't touch that. I don't have the negative."

Kate turned at Sam's anxious voice. She stood in the doorway of the kitchen, holding a bottle of red wine.

"You still have it."

"Please," Sam asked again, her eyes pleading. "Please don't touch it. It's the only picture I have of the two of us."

"You do still love him. Susan and Javi were right. Nothing really ended, did it?" Kate whispered. She saw tears prick Sam's eyes.

"What do you want, Kate? Why are you here?" Her questions tumbled out in a rush. "You want to know how I feel about Reed?"

"Yes," Kate breathed out.

Sam cleared her throat. Shaking her head and setting the wine bottle down, she crossed her arms and stared out the windows at the lake for a moment. Then she glanced around the kitchen, her gaze finally coming to rest on the old refrigerator covered by black and white snapshots.

"Fine. Come on then. It's sort of hard to put into words for me," Sam said quietly before she walked down the hall.

As they walked toward the living room, Kate looked at the art lining the walls. "Do you have any of Reed's photographs?"

Sam paused when she got near the front door. "Sure I do," she murmured. "He still sends me flowers." She nodded toward a small reading corner Kate hadn't looked into. It was tucked into the corner of the room and set off by floor to ceiling bookcases. When she walked around the corner, she gasped.

Lining the back wall was a series of framed black and white prints. There were at least a dozen, maybe more, and each picture showed a large familiar hand holding a palmful of flowers. Roses, pansies, a single lily. Every picture held a different flower, but every hand was the same.

Kate's breath caught in her throat. "How many?"

"Fifteen," Sam said quietly. "I was surprised the first time I got one. It was on my birthday. I'd heard he was dating some dancer, but he sent a picture anyway." She blinked tears away and swallowed. "It was nice of him to remember."

"Sam, I really think—"

"The studio's upstairs. There's good light up there. Just..." Kate heard Sam pause then laugh a little. "Just give me a second, okay?"

"Okay, sure."

"Just—give me a minute," Sam said. "I'll call when it's ready."

She walked up the stairs and Kate felt her phone vibrate in her pocket; looking at the screen, she answered with a smile.

"Hey." She walked back toward the wall of flowers. "Yeah, I'm here now... no she's been nice." Kate paused again to listen. "I should be home by then."

She walked back toward the front door and stared out the window at the sun reflecting off the lake. "Yeah, tell Mari I'll be there."

Kate heard Sam call from upstairs. "Come on up, Kate."

She moved toward the staircase. "I need to go. I'll call you when I'm heading down the mountain." She paused and a grin spread across her face. "Yeah? Well, I'll look forward to that, handsome. Bye!" She clicked off the phone when she heard the loud grumble start on the other end of the line. Kate chuckled and started up the stairs.

At the top, she stepped into a large, open room Sam used as a studio. Large windows were open to the surrounding trees, and it smelled faintly of acrylic paint and lemon. Small metal paint tubes were tossed in a colorful heap on a work table in the corner; brushes dried in bunches, stuffed into mason jars which decorated work tables and windowsills, reminding Kate of odd, prickly flower arrangements. She noticed that drop-cloths and sheets covered a number of the canvases, and several others were propped backward against the walls.

"So, here it is."

The paintings she could see were a combination of colorful landscapes Sam must have been working on, and canvas after canvas of Reed O'Connor.

There were portraits and vignettes in various stages of completion. She saw one of Reed smiling and holding a camera in a park. A picture of the photographer sleeping in a corner of their studio in New York. Still another was a painting of him in bed, grinning with one arm thrown over his eyes. Kate also saw numerous anatomy studies: an arm, a brilliant blue eye, or the muscles of a defined back.

"These are amazing." Kate nodded toward one of the draped canvases. "Are these unfinished or something?"

Sam smirked. "Well, I figured there might be a few pictures of Reed you didn't want to see."

"Oh?" Understanding dawned. "Oh! Yeah, that's okay." Kate blushed.

"Let's just say, if you want to ever be able to look at him the same way..." Sam winked. "I mean, if you want a peek—"

"No! No, that's okay. Really."

"Are you sure? He's pretty spectacular. I'm sure Javi won't mind. It's *art*, you know." Sam winked and moved her hand to one particularly large canvas covered by a white sheet. "Research and all that."

Kate knew she was beet-red. "No! Really, thanks anyway."

Sam chuckled before turning around to survey her work.

"Wow," Kate whispered as she looked around.

Reed was right. Sam Rhodes's portrait work was stunning. Kate wandered among the canvases.

"Are these all from memory?"

Sam nodded. "I left all my sketch books in New York. I think I've done pretty well. I..." She paused, taking a deep breath and blinking rapidly. "When I left, I destroyed all my paintings of him. I regretted it immediately. I wasn't well. And I had such an erratic temper. I've been trying to recreate some of them over the past year or so. I want to try doing portraits again, so I thought I'd start with him." Sam smiled gently and traced a finger over the length of Reed's arm on the canvas in front of her. "It's kind of like my own personal therapy."

Kate saw Sam bite her lip as she tried to control her emotions. "You see, that night—the night I left—was when I really messed things up. I'd been depressed before, but that night I said a lot of really horrible things to him." Sam cleared her throat, and Kate saw a tear slip down her cheek.

"Is that—"

"That's why we're not together anymore, Kate. It's not really anything he did, it's because I was messed up. And no matter how much he loved me, Reed couldn't fix me. And however much you might wish for one, there's no rewind button on your mouth."

Kate frowned. "But, you can apologize, can't you?"

"Yeah, I can." Sam wiped her cheek. "But by the time I was better—*really* better—he was pretty angry with me, and I can't blame him for that."

"But don't you think—"

"He's got his own life now." Sam shook her head. "I don't want to mess it up again."

Kate sighed. "You know, I really think he would still listen."

Sam shrugged. "It's a little like watercolors, isn't it? One wrong stroke... those brush marks don't go away. You can try to cover them up, but once that paint is down, it's not like you can erase it, is it? Those words can't be unsaid." She shook her head. "I'm sure he's forgiven me in his own way, and I forgave him for anything he might have done to me a long time ago, but he's moved on. And that's good. He deserves that."

"Sam—"

"I know you don't want to think this at age twenty-four," Sam squared her shoulders and faced her. "But some things can't be fixed." She shook her head with tears in her eyes. "It just doesn't work that way. Not everything broken can be put back together, and sometimes the best you can do is treasure your memories and try to move on."

Sam looked around the studio with tears sliding down her face, and Kate glared at her, frustration finally bubbling to the surface.

"Are you serious?" she hissed. "Do you really believe that? You just let go of a love like that and let him 'move on?' Reed hasn't 'moved on' any more than you have." She looked around the room littered with ghosts.

"He lives in that studio by himself like a damn hermit, Sam. He's still hung up on you, and then I come here, and find out you're completely hung up on him, too."

Kate thought about the last five months of her life and the cluster of miscommunication she'd stepped into. She almost had the urge to stomp her foot. She glared at Sam. "Don't you people talk to each other? I'm barely twenty-four, and I know you need to *talk to each other*. You were all willing to talk to me like I'm some sort of confessor, but none of you are talking to each other. It's ridiculous!"

Sam sat stunned, staring at the young woman in front of her, whose anger was growing by the minute. "You mean—"

"And you say that love is like... what? A *watercolor* painting? 'The brushstrokes don't disappear?' Well, I'm sorry, but that's bullshit. Life isn't a painting."

Sam just stared at her, her eyes narrowed as she watched the young woman. "I think you need to tell me—"

"But you know what?" Kate's eyes darted around the room full of canvases. "If it was a painting, it wouldn't be a watercolor, that's for sure. It would be like a—an oil painting. You can fix those, right?"

Sam nodded. "Yeah, you—"

"You layer them and correct the mistakes." Kate nodded and pointed at one partially finished painting of Reed in profile. "Then the brushstrokes become part of the work, not a mistake. And sure, they take forever to dry, but once they do, they last forever."

"I guess that's—"

"That's the kind of love *I* want; and that's the kind of love you guys could have. Because you still love him. And I know he still loves you. So, just... just fix it." Kate walked over and stood in front of Sam. Tears filled the painter's eyes, and Kate looked at her with pleading expression.

"Sam, the man practically has a shrine to you in his studio. Not a creepy one, more of a 'I'm totally in love with this woman' one. And for heaven's sake..." Kate walked over, pointing to one of the canvases of a young Reed clothed only in a pair of blue jeans and holding a camera with a passionate look on his face. "Look at him! He's *gorgeous*. And brilliant and—and thinks you walk on water! I mean... are you nuts?"

Sam cracked a sharp laugh, then immediately covered her mouth in shock. Kate stared back, suddenly realizing her word choice may have not been ideal. "That may have not been the best way to phrase it."

Sam stared at her with wide eyes and a hand still covering her mouth.

Kate felt horrible. "Listen, Sam, I'm sorry, I just—"

"What do you mean, 'he has a shrine?'"

CHAPTER TWENTY-SEVEN

Pomona, California
September 2010

Javi traced the line of Kate's side as she slept next to him. His fingers slid along the dip of her waist before rising gently at her hip, finally drifting off along her narrow thigh. He marveled at the juxtaposition of her pale skin against his brightly colored arms, and scowled at the calluses on his hands, frustrated he often marked her without meaning to.

If she was awake, she would smooth the line between his eyebrows and tease him about worrying too much. If she was awake, she would say something outrageous to make him laugh. If she was awake, she would kiss him as she lay across his chest, stealing his breath and reminding Javi that, despite appearances, *he* was the breakable one.

"Javi…" she murmured in her sleep. Her waves of red-gold hair lay spread along his shoulder, and he brushed away a piece that was tickling her nose. The early morning light poured into the bedroom and made her skin glow.

"Yeah?" he whispered.

"There's no cat in the warehouse," she mumbled.

His shoulders shook with silent laughter at her sleepy conversation. He'd been delighted weeks ago to discover how much she talked in her sleep. "No, Katie, no cat in the warehouse."

"But a cat wouldn't eat snakes."

He struggled to hold in the snort.

"No snakes in the warehouse, either."

"Oh." She sighed. "Okay."

He stared at her freckled face for a few more minutes before he finally whispered the question he'd been asking her for weeks, almost every morning before she woke.

"You love me, Katie?"

"Uh-huh." She breathed out with a smile and snuggled closer into his side.

"I love you, too," he whispered before he kissed her forehead and closed his eyes again. They slept for another hour, her limbs draped over his body as she clung to him in her dreams. He woke before her, this time watching her until her blue eyes flickered open.

"Morning," he muttered, a small smile teasing the corner of his mouth from the memory of her sleepy confession.

Kate blinked rapidly and buried her face in his neck as if hiding from the bright light. "What time is it?"

"Around eight, I think."

"We've got plenty of time." She peeled herself away from him, arching like a cat in his large bed. "Have I told you lately how much I like your bed? So much room to stretch." She let out a yawn.

Smiling, Javi rolled over in bed, caging her under him and kissing along her neck.

"That better not be the only reason," he said between kisses.

Kate laughed and tried to squirm away, but his teasing kisses quickly turned into something more, and then she was the one pulling him closer.

"Not the only reason," she purred as his mouth explored her body. Her hands gripped his shoulders, digging in and holding him tightly. "Javi," she whispered his name before his mouth covered her own. His hand sneaked around to the small of her back and pulled her closer as she wrapped her legs around his hips, and they rocked together in the tangled sheets.

He sat up, pulling her with him and turning her around so he could see the flaming hair fall down her back. Javi brushed it to the side and wrapped his arms around her, cupping her breasts as he buried his face in her warm neck and tasted her skin.

"What do you want?" he breathed out as they rocked together. His hands slid down her body. "Tell me what you need."

"You."

185

His breath caught for a moment before his mouth closed over her skin. His teeth nipped at the curve of her shoulder, and he pressed their bodies together.

"Just you."

He teased the soft skin at the juncture of her thighs, spreading her before he slid inside. Kate let out a soft cry and Javi softened his hands, sliding them over her body in long, lazy strokes as they made love. He sat back and trailed kisses along the curve of her spine as he felt her heart race against his palm.

"Talented," she gasped. "*Really* talented hands."

"Shhh," he said. "I'm a professional. Let me work."

Javi wrapped his arms around her waist and pulled her harder onto his body. He bit his lip when Kate let out a moan, and her head fell back on his shoulder as he sped up. He quickly worked her into a frenzy until Kate was arching back and gripping his arms. She clenched around him and cried out in release as he surged forward, closing his eyes and biting his lip hard as he came. Then he fell forward with a satisfied groan and rolled them to the side, still peppering her back with kisses as her breathing evened out.

Perfect, he thought. She was perfect.

Actually, she was a nosey, stubborn, pain in the ass.

And she was perfect.

What a surprise. He smiled and wrapped her up in his arms.

Hours later, they still lay in bed, Javi on his stomach and Kate straddling his back, trying to give him a massage. He had been welding for three days straight, but had promised her he would take a full weekend off so she wouldn't have to go to her parent's Labor Day party alone.

"Your back is impossible," she grumbled as she tried to knead the thick muscles covering his shoulders. "I feel like I need a jackhammer to even make a dent in it."

Javi smirked. He always enjoyed her hands on him, even if she wasn't giving a very good massage. "Just lean in. Use your elbows."

"Won't that hurt?"

"No," he chuckled. "I don't think you'll bruise me."

Kate leaned onto his back with the full weight of her tiny frame. She was so light, he could barely feel her, and his shoulders shook with laughter.

"You know what? Never mind." She slapped his back. "Find some scary woman named Helga with a unibrow to beat on your muscles, old man."

"Hey."

She giggled a little and bent down to nip his ear with her teeth. "Wait here, handsome."

Javi felt her move off of him, and the bed shifted when she left. He lay, dozing a little, until she came back, but woke when he heard the familiar zip of her camera bag. He grumbled out a warning, "Katie…"

"Just your back. I want pictures of your back. The light's really good right now."

He grunted, but lay still as she began to take pictures of him wrapped in the white sheets. He knew she would never use anything without asking him. And since he had plans to sketch her for a piece himself, Javi knew he could hardly complain.

"Why did you get the phoenix on your back?" She began her typical string of questions as she changed the lens and fiddled with her camera. He thought about the fierce bird that covered his back from hip to neck. The curling red wings were so large they dipped over his shoulders in front.

"Flames, welding, ashes, phoenix. It all just seemed to go together." He paused for a moment. "It reminds me that… sometimes things need to burn to get better. In life. In art. Beautiful things can come from ashes. And sometimes, the fire that looks like it's destroying really just makes things stronger. That's it, I guess."

She was silent for a long moment before he heard the click of her camera again. He peeked over his shoulder.

"Do you like my tattoos?"

"I have to fight the urge to trace every single one of them with my tongue," she said as she continued snapping pictures. "What do you think?"

He grinned. "I think you shouldn't fight the urge. And you're trying to turn me on again."

"Yeah, 'cause that's such a challenge." She laughed and continued capturing frame after frame of his intricately decorated skin. They were both silent as she worked, and he drifted in and out of sleep.

"What should I wear to this thing?" he asked, clearing his throat a little.

"Sadly, clothes." She muttered something unintelligible about angles and shadows.

"Not kidding, Katie."

She frowned when he rolled over to look at her. She shoved him back. "Neither am I—hold still. Wear whatever. I don't care. It's on the water, and it'll be cool when the sun goes down, so maybe bring a jacket."

Shaking his head, Javi marveled at how accepting she was of his intrusion on her privileged world. He'd met her parents weeks ago at a dinner Chris and Dee hosted for Kate to celebrate the completion of her degree. The Mitchells were understandably wary of the man twelve years older than their daughter, who she'd jumped into a relationship with after breaking up with her boyfriend of four years. Javi's brusque demeanor, scores of tattoos, and background in East L.A. probably didn't help, either.

"Roll over to the side... there." He shook his head and let her move his arms to a different angle.

"How much long—"

"Shhhh."

Javi had to give Dee and Chris a lot of credit for making him sound nicer than he actually was. Shannon Mitchell, being the good Irish mother that she was, was somewhat comforted by the fact Javi had been raised a staunch Catholic and still saw his mother regularly. Derrick Mitchell seemed more impressed by Javi's background working at his father's auto body shop than by the sculptures he had seen downtown with his name on them.

"Almost... oh, wait, let me try this filter."

"Kate, I am not a prop."

"Well, you kind of are." She placated him with a kiss on his rough cheek. "Only *my* prop, though."

Despite the months they'd been together, Kate's father still watched him with clear suspicion. Considering the thoughts Javi entertained about the man's daughter almost constantly, he couldn't really blame him.

Javi knew that Kate's parents had nothing to worry about. Though his surly demeanor hadn't altered, he was absolutely crazy about their daughter. He couldn't remember a time when he'd been happier, even though he still couldn't figure out why she wanted to be with him. He sure as hell wasn't going to argue with her about it, even though she was cute when she was pissed off. For Kate's sake, Javi hoped her parents would eventually see how much he admired and respected her, but he wasn't going to worry about it. Kate seemed content, and since she was the only one Javi gave a shit about, that was all he really needed.

"Just letting you know, I think the douchebag will be at the barbecue with his mom and dad," she said as she continued snapping pictures.

Javi immediately rolled over, despite her protests, and pulled her on top of him.

"Hey!"

"Oh really?" he asked with an evil grin, his eyes lighting up. "The douchebag?"

"He's not even worth your time."

He set her camera carefully to the side, making sure not to smudge the lens. He turned back to her and tucked a piece of hair behind her ear. "I know, but it's the principle. I'll make sure to wear something that shows off my ink. He'll probably think I'm in a gang... yo."

She rolled her eyes and pinched his shoulder. "Whatever you want to do. Honestly, when he sees you, he'll probably pee his pants no matter what you wear."

"That's always nice to hear."

"You know..."

He frowned. "What?"

Kate reached up, and her fingers traced along his jaw, which was covered with three days' worth of stubble.

"I don't even think about him anymore. I was more embarrassed than hurt by him cheating on me."

Javi shrugged. "His loss, my gain. All that shit."

Her mouth curled into a smile, and she leaned down to kiss him before she laid her head over his heart.

"My gain," she whispered.

Javi felt his throat catch for a second, and he ran rough hands down the length of her back. "Our gain."

CHAPTER TWENTY-EIGHT

Crestline, California
September 2010

Sam stared at the black and white pictures littering her refrigerator. Most had come in the first six months after she moved back to California, though Reed would still send her one occasionally. They weren't accompanied by a note, but she always knew who had taken them. He never took landscapes or cityscapes for work, but he'd taken pictures of most of her favorite places in the city to send to her in California.

Looking now, Sam realized that there was a small piece of Reed in each of the frames.

One had the toe of his black boot sticking into a picture of her favorite bench in Prospect Park. One caught a glimpse of his reflection in the glass door of her morning coffee shop in Williamsburg. But the one she stared at now had arrived in the mail six months after she had left and right before Reed's messages got angry.

It was a picture of their bed in the apartment; the white sheets were rumpled in the morning sun, and his long arm stretched across the empty space where she had once slept. His hand was clutching the sheets. For the first time, Sam felt like she truly grasped what he'd been trying to tell her, though she was too distraught to understand at the time.

Sam reached up and pulled the picture off the fridge, touching the hand in the picture and wishing she had the real one to hold. If what Kate said was true, they had wasted years. And if what Kate said was true, Sam was determined to find her way back.

She heard the doorbell ring, and set her glass of water and the picture down to go answer it. She was expecting a delivery of oil paints to arrive that day and was glad UPS was early.

When she opened the door, she choked and stumbled back, stunned by the familiar face standing on the other side of the screen.

It was Reed.

Her eyes drank him in as she clutched the door. His dark hair was short, though it still curled at the tips. His mouth was set in a serious line, and his hands rested nervously in the pockets of his jeans as his foot tapped on the porch.

"Hi," he whispered.

She gaped, unable to speak, and a barrage of memories overwhelmed her at the sound of his voice.

He was the cocky boy smirking at her from a couch. *"You're looking at me like you're imagining me naked, so I thought you might be, well... imagining me naked."*

The desperate man waking from a fevered dream. *"Am I dreaming?"*

A tender lover with his hand on her shoulder. *"I love you."*

An agonized partner in a cold hospital room. *"I don't know what I'd do if I lost you."*

Reed frowned, fidgeting on the front porch, but Sam was still frozen in shock, holding her arms around her body as if to keep herself from flying apart.

He spoke again. "So obviously, this is a surprise. I, um... I don't really know what I'm doing here." He sighed. "No, that's not true." He scowled and his hand reached up to grab the back of his neck. "You see, I got a note from a certain grad student we both know." He paused for a moment, continuing when he saw that she still couldn't speak. "Want to see it?"

He didn't wait for her response, but reached into his pocket to pull out a folded piece of notebook paper. He carefully unfolded and spread it open, holding it so Sam could see it through the screen door. There were only five words:

She still has the picture.

Sam's breath caught in a quiet cry as she read the note, and she felt tears prick the corners of her eyes. Her hands touched the paper through the screen, and she looked up at Reed's face, familiar, yet still changed by the years they had been apart.

He cleared his throat and stared down at his shoe as it kicked a loose nail on the porch. Her fingers itched to reach through the door and smooth the lines that time and stress had etched around his eyes.

"I guess I just need to know why you still have it, because…" He paused for a moment before continuing in a low voice. "I lost mine. I mean… I destroyed it. See, once upon a time, I didn't realize what I had. And I lost the right light for a minute. In one very foolish moment, I tore up something that meant everything to me."

Sam's mouth formed his name, but she still couldn't find her voice.

Reed cleared his throat before he continued. "So, I tried to tape it up, but I could only find scraps. And the scraps didn't make much of a picture."

Fat tears rolled down her face, and Sam leaned forward to push the screen door open. Reed stepped back and let her walk out. His eyes were red and glassy, and his voice was soft as he watched her.

"I found the painting you started. I kept that. I hung it on the wall in the studio, even though it's not finished. But I can remember, you know? Fill in the rest when I look at it hard enough."

Reed lifted a tentative hand to touch her cheek, and his fingers traced the line of her jaw. "And it's beautiful, Sammy, but I miss the real thing. And when I got this note, I thought maybe I could see it again." He swallowed audibly before continuing in a hoarse whisper, "Or maybe just—"

"Reed," she finally choked out. Sam reached for his hand, brushing her tears away before she stepped forward and wrapped her arms around his waist. He caught her, holding tightly as she soaked up the feel of him. She felt like she could breathe again.

"I missed you so much," he whispered.

He held her as her tears stained his shirt. Sam didn't try to hide them. She just clutched him tighter, letting her tears wash away the years of separation. Finally, Reed picked her up and carried her to the steps of the old porch. He sat down and Sam straddled his lap, still clinging to him. His arms held her as her tears slowed and the tension drained from her body.

He wiped his own eyes on his shoulders, never letting his arms leave her waist. Sam sniffed, exhaling shaky breaths into his chest. Then she allowed herself to bury her face in his neck and breathe in the scent of him. Soap. Sweat. The unique and familiar smell of his skin. Home. Even after all the years apart, Reed still smelled like home.

"I've always had that picture," she said. "Always."

His callused hands lifted to frame her face as his eyes drank her in. Reed kissed her forehead, and Sam closed her eyes and smiled. Working his way down, he kissed each eyelid, the swells of her cheeks and the tip of her nose. He tilted her head so his lips could place soft kisses along her jawline leading toward her ear.

"I love you," he whispered. "I never stopped. Please, believe me."

She reached her hands up to weave her fingers with his own. "I never stopped either. I love you so much."

Their mouths met, their bodies entwined, and their lips moved against each other as if they had never been apart. She ran her fingers up his neck to stroke his hair, pulling him closer, gasping a little as his mouth left hers to taste her neck.

"I missed you," he whispered as her eyes closed in pleasure. "So much. Every night. I dream about you every night."

She pulled him even closer and whispered between hungry kisses, "Some days, I felt like I could hardly breathe."

Finally pausing to catch his breath, Reed leaned his forehead on hers, caging her in his arms. "We have to go back. My life? It wasn't... it just *wasn't*."

Sam shook her head and smoothed the lines between his eyes.

"We can't go back, Reed. Even as much as we both want to." She continued quickly when she saw his look of panic. "But I think—I think maybe we can move forward."

Part Eleven:
The Mirror

CHAPTER TWENTY-NINE

Pomona, California
November 2010

"He's not boring."

"He's completely boring, Kate."

"No, he's not. He just has better manners than you."

Javi scowled at her. "You like it that I don't have manners."

"I don't *like* it. I just like you. The fact that you have no manners is kind of unimportant, except when you're talking to my mother."

He shrugged. "I'm nice to the people who matter."

Kate snorted and reached her hand across the seat to smack his thigh. Javi grabbed it and pulled her small hand to rest on his lap. "You know," Kate started, "if it hadn't been for Professor Chris, I wouldn't have ever met you, Javi."

He stared at her for a long moment. "Fine. I'll be nice, but you've got to stop calling him Professor Chris. It sounds weird. He's Chris. Boring Chris."

"Does Boring Chris make Wonderful Dee happy?"

Kate knew Javi had a huge soft spot for the tiny photographer, and she saw his hard expression relax in the intermittent light of the street lamps.

"Yes," he muttered.

"Okay then. Just be polite."

"Kate?"

"Mmmhmm?"

"Are Chris and Dee our 'couple friends' now?"

She had to hold back her snort when she saw his lip curl. Instead she plastered an innocent look on her face. "I don't know. Are we a couple?"

His head swung around and his eyebrows drew together in a frown. "What the hell?"

"I don't know. We've been... whatever we are, for four months now, but you've never asked me to be your girlfriend."

He glared at her. "Are you being serious right now?"

She repressed her smile. She was mostly joking. There was no doubt in her mind Javi considered them committed to each other, but she could also confess a small, juvenile part of her wanted to hear Javi call her his girlfriend.

The longer they were together, the more things seemed to fall into place for Kate. Javi was one of the smartest people she had ever met and one of the most talented. He was respectful but challenging in exactly the ways she needed. Being with him filled a hole in her life she didn't even know she had.

And she also had to admit that she was fascinated by him. She loved tracing the hard planes and angles of his body, transfixed by the shadows they created. She would lay next to him while he slept and stare at the large phoenix adorning his back, trying to imagine what moment had inspired each tattoo that covered his body. Someday, she wanted to know the story behind each one, whether it was happy or sad.

For some reason, at that moment sitting in the car next to him, what Javi had said all those months ago at the art walk finally made sense.

"Oh!" she said with a small laugh.

He looked at her as she drove the old pickup.

"What? You're joking with me, right?"

She grinned at him. "I don't need a nice guy."

"What?"

She needed *him*. He was rude, gruff, and mostly lacking in manners. He was brilliant and intense. He saw her in a way that Cody had never seen her in all the time they had known each other. He'd seen her from the beginning. And despite the years and circumstances that separated them, she had seen him, too.

"One frame?"

"One frame to capture who you think I am."

It was the same one Kate would pick today, highlighting his stubborn jaw, his strangely graceful collarbone, and the star-like scars that dotted his thick neck.

Kate glanced at him and realized she had never answered his question and he was now glaring at her. She pulled over to the side of the road and put the truck in park.

Turning to him, she leaned across the cab of his pickup truck and kissed the cheek she hadn't been able to convince him to shave. She smiled as her lips met rough stubble.

"Javier Lugo," she asked simply, "will you be my boyfriend?"

She was pretty sure his face was red, despite the darkness of the truck cab, and she snickered a little.

"You're cute when you blush, old man."

Grunting, he turned and reached an arm around her waist, dragging her to straddle his lap as his other hand grasped the back of her neck and he pulled her in for a searing kiss. He devoured her mouth and pressed her body into his so she could feel how much he wanted her.

She only pulled him closer, arching against his chest when his hands gripped the small of her back.

They were lost in each other, ignoring the traffic that whizzed by on the busy street. When he finally let her up for air, she panted, but still held him close.

"Don't," he said as he continued to bite along her neck and behind her ear, "call your boyfriend an 'old man.'" He paused and looked at her with a smirk. "It's bad manners."

She pinched his ear as he laughed and crawled off his lap to the driver's seat again.

"We're going to be late."

He shrugged. "It's Dee and Chris. They don't care. They're our 'couple friends' now."

Kate laughed as she put the car in drive and pulled back onto the road heading toward the Bradley's house in Claremont. After a minute, she heard Javi's phone ring. Fishing it out of his pocket, he flipped it open.

"Hey, man, what's up?"

She guessed from the friendly tone of voice it was probably Reed, who was still staying in the mountains at Sam's cabin. Kate had been thrilled to hear he had flown out to California after receiving her note, and Susan had called her last month to tell her she thought Sam and Reed were working things out. Judging from

Reed's loud voice on the phone, she imagined there might be a few bumps in their happily ever after.

"Reed, I don't know what to tell you." Javi paused. "I'm sure she thought she was doing the right thing. Wouldn't you try to protect her if you thought—" He scowled as his friend interrupted him.

Kate continued driving, turning onto the small residential street where Chris and Dee lived.

"Oh, no. Turn your damn car around and drive back to that cabin, asshole. If I come home with my girlfriend to find your drunk ass sitting on my porch again, I'm going to kick you back to New York, and you won't be near as pretty when you get there."

She grinned when she heard him call her his girlfriend, even if it wasn't in the most romantic context, but she had to laugh a little, too. They had found Reed sitting on Javi's porch a couple of weeks ago, drunk and pissed off, when Javi and Kate came back from dinner at his sister's restaurant. Within the hour, Reed had been talking with Sam on the phone again, and she had driven down the mountain to pick him up, looking more than a little embarrassed.

"Do I look like Dr. Phil? Work this shit out, Reed." His voice lowered and took on a more serious tone. "You two have dealt with worse... just work it out, man." He paused again and Kate heard Reed's voice, calmer and sounding more collected. "Yeah... call me tomorrow. Not too early."

She parked in front of Chris and Dee's house and waited for him to finish his call. When he finally snapped the phone shut, he turned and looked at her with a grimace.

"I am not Dr. Phil."

She shook her head seriously. "No, you're not. You still have all your hair... for now."

He just rolled his eyes and walked over to grab her hand. Suddenly, he stopped on the walkway and pulled her in for a fierce embrace.

"Javi—"

"Please don't ever try to protect me by not telling me things, Katie," he said quietly. "Do you understand?" He pulled away and looked into her wide blue eyes. "I don't ever want you to not tell me if something's not okay." He frowned as he smoothed a strand of hair away from her face to tuck behind her ear.

"Fair enough. Same to you."

Frowning a little, he nodded. "I know we're not... I mean, we're not them, but—"

Kate cut him off with a gentle kiss. "Nothing wrong with learning from your friends."

Javi cupped her cheeks with his hands and placed a lingering kiss on her lips before he backed away, taking her hand in his and walking up the path.

"Boring Chris." He sighed. "He's going to end up talking all night about the thrill of capturing the two-toed horny woodpecker in its natural habitat or some shit like that."

Kate suppressed her laugh. "Shut up and be polite, you cranky old man."

CHAPTER THIRTY

Crestline, California
November 2010

Reed could see her bundled in a blanket and sitting on the end of the dock when he pulled back into the clearing in front of the cabin. His immediate thought was that it was too cold for her to be sitting on the water like that, but then he imagined the scathing comment she would make about him being "overprotective" and decided not to say anything.

Instead, he walked up to the porch and grabbed another blanket before walking out to join her. When he got close enough, she turned and he could see the tear tracks on her cheeks.

"I thought you were going to Javi's."

"He said he'd kick me out if I showed up. I think he likes Kate more than me now."

Reed saw Sam's mouth curl up a bit at the corner, and he went to settle next to her. Instead of sitting, he lay down on his back with his head almost at the edge of the dock so he could look into her face while he looked at the stars.

"I'm sorry," she said, looking down at him. "I should have told you."

"I'm sorry, too. I hate to think of you going through that alone."

"I wasn't al—"

"Sam," he bit out. "You're making excuses." It hadn't been her cousin's responsibility to help her through her depression. It had been his, and it was going to be a while before he wasn't mad at her for hiding it from him.

He had spent their first week back together apologizing for kissing another woman, something he still felt guilty about, but it wasn't until she had confessed the depression to him that Reed had felt the true cost of their separation. He felt concern first, then a resurgence of grief, and tonight he had finally reached anger.

"How would *you* feel, Sam? If you knew I had gone through something like that and not allowed you to help me?"

"I'd be angry," she whispered, nodding as she looked across the cold lake. "I'd be—"

"Furious. You'd be absolutely furious."

She sighed. "I know."

They both stared into the dark night around them as they processed their thoughts.

"I can't apologize anymore, Reed. I can't. I feel like we're going through the same arguments over and over. I messed up. You messed up. We both messed up. A lot. We're both guilty. We both assumed things. We're both stubborn about listening to our friends. So what do we do? Do you want to move past this? Or is this it?"

He frowned. "What?"

"You heard me. We have to forgive each other… *really* forgive each other, or just say goodbye."

"Forget that," he snorted.

"What?"

Reed reached up to grab her chin so she had to look at him. "I lived four years without you like some kind of zombie. I'm not letting you go again. We were both miserable."

"Fine." She reached down to frame his face with both hands. "Then I forgive you, Reed O'Connor. For everything. And I apologize for hiding things from you, and for running away instead of trusting you. And I don't want to ever bring it up again."

He placed one large hand on hers to hold it to his cheek when he responded. "I forgive you," he said in a hoarse voice. "And I'm sorry for breaking our trust in a foolish moment. I'm sorry for letting you go too easily and not seeing what you were going through. And I don't ever want to bring it up again, either."

"Okay."

"Okay… but you have to promise not to hide stuff from me."

"And you have to promise not to wrap me up in protective packaging when you get scared."

He nodded. "I can do that."

"Okay. No hiding stuff. And no bubble wrap."

"Sounds fair." He finally smiled. "I love you."

"I love you, too."

They sat quietly in the moonlight for a while longer, Reed cradling Sam's hand against his face as he looked at the stars, and Sam staring out at the dark tree line.

"I want you to move back to New York," he whispered.

Sam looked at him and tried to pull her hand away, but he pressed his hand over hers more securely and refused to let her break contact.

"You came here to heal," he persisted. "You've healed. Don't you think it's time to move forward?"

"I love this place," Sam blinked the tears from her eyes. "I have a life here. I have family, I have—"

"You're alone. Hiding. Just like I've been." He sat up and angled his shoulders toward her. "You're in the middle of nowhere, and I'm surrounded by people, but we're both still alone. You love this place? Fine, we'll come back. We'll spend summers here. God knows it's nicer than Manhattan in August. But Sam"—He hugged her to his chest—"aren't you ready for the people again?"

She closed her eyes and leaned into his embrace. Reed's memory flashed through a thousand mental pictures of her in the city they had loved. Sam laughing with Lydia in a cafe wearing a cappuccino foam mustache. Sketching a busker in the subway as the musician danced and grinned. Sitting with an old man, smiling and tossing crumbs for pigeons in Central Park as Reed snapped pictures. He remembered flashes of her stretched out on the bed in their studio as the afternoon sun poured in through the high windows and made her skin glow like she was lit from within.

Reed held her, willing her to remember as he did. "Please, Sam, I need you back. I *can't* go back without you."

Finally, her hand lifted and stroked his temple, as if maybe she could see the pictures in his mind's eye. He held her close, relaxing into the anchor of her touch. Reed felt her pull away from him, but her hand remained stroking his hair. When he finally looked her in the eye, he smiled.

"Yeah," Sam said, "I think… maybe I am ready."

CHAPTER THIRTY-ONE

Pomona, California
March 2011

"Katie!"

Javi called toward the back corner where he had seen Kate heading to work.

"Yeah?" she called back.

"Where are you?"

"In the back by the pipes. Why?"

He rounded the corner where he saw the glow from the light kits she had set up. Kate was in the corner sitting inside a giant concrete pipe he had salvaged from a building site. She was curled up and only wearing a thin t-shirt and a pair of panties with the camera trained on her. He uttered a muffled groan when he saw her; his reaction toward her bare skin as strong as the first time he'd seen it, eight months before.

She sat up in surprise as she spotted him out of the corner of her eye. "Hey," she called, but the movement left her off balance, and she toppled over backward.

"Oh, shit!" she cried.

Javi rushed forward, panicked by her sudden fall. "Kate?"

He heard her small voice from behind the pipes. "I'm okay. I pulled a mattress back here 'cause it happened before. I'm not hurt. Just... sort of stuck."

Relief flooded him when he heard her, quickly overtaken by the hilarity of the situation, as he burst into laughter.

"It happened before?" he gasped. "What have you been doing back here?"

"It's that layering thing I was talking about. I do the same pose wearing… you know what, just shut up and help me get out of here."

Still laughing, he looked around where she had her equipment set up. He was hoping the camera was on a timer and had captured that fall.

"Uh…Javi? A little help, please?"

"Yeah, I'm working on it. Do you have a blanket or something? So you don't scratch your legs up?" Marring her perfect legs would be a crime.

"No. I have my jeans over there, but there's not really room to put them on, I'm sort of wedged—"

"Okay, just…" Still snickering, he walked over and peeked through the pipe to the other side where Kate was wedged between the corrugated wall and the pipe. "Hi there."

"At least you didn't call the ambulance this time."

"I just *thought* about calling them, Katie. I didn't actually do it. And thought you had stabbed yourself with rebar."

"As fascinating as this conversation is, can you maybe get me out of here?"

"Hold on," he muttered.

Javi climbed into the pipe and reached a hand down for her to take. She didn't appear to be hurt, but there was no way she would have been able to climb out herself.

"I think you can just grab onto my arm and—"

"Yeah, I think I have it. It's a good thing you're so strong," she said breathlessly.

Feeling a little bit like Superman, he felt her fingers wrap around his bicep, and he tried grasping her arm, only to brush up against what felt a lot like a pert breast. He heard her let out a soft whimper, and he let his fingers wander. "Hmm, is it cold in here?"

"Help me out and I'll let you know, you perv."

"You're so mean to me." He laughed. "Here, just grab on. Both hands…"

"Okay, I think I have it." Javi heard her grunt before she grasped his arm firmly, and he pulled her up toward him as he braced himself in the pipe. He lifted her with one tug, so she was lying soft, warm, and almost naked in his arms.

Well, that worked out better than expected.

Kate's legs lay across his own and her right arm came up to grasp his shoulder. They were both breathing heavily, and he felt his hands grip, as if he was keeping her from escaping. Their faces were only inches apart as they sat curled in the pipe, and he could feel her warm breath on his cheek.

"Hey," he said, looking at her lips as her tongue darted out to lick them.

"Hey yourself." She wiggled on his lap and Javi groaned.

"Clumsy, stubborn little girl..." He slowly drew her closer, and his callused hands trailed down her smooth shoulders, grazing the sides of her breasts before they rested at her waist. Kate shivered, but he only smiled, enjoying his playful seduction.

"Cranky, bossy old man..."

"You gonna say thank you?" Javi's head tilted slightly, and he saw her eyes dart down to his mouth before her lips reached up to meet his own in a burning kiss.

He was surrounded by her, his right hand reached up to grasp the hair at the nape of her neck and his fingers flexed in the warm flame. His other hand gripped her waist, dragging her into his chest. Her hands moved from his solid shoulders, up toward his neck, and she pulled him closer, pressing her body against his. Javi inhaled her soft breath and stroked her tongue when she opened to him. A soft whimper escaped her throat, and he backed away from her, only to have her pull his mouth back to hers.

"Katie," he murmured, as her lips left his to trail along his jaw. Her swollen mouth nibbled at his jaw, and her hands reached down his neck to spread under his t-shirt as she scratched her nails along his skin. "I swear I came back to tell you something and not just rescue you from your own photograph and fool around."

"Thanks, by the way."

"You're very welcome."

"Javi?" she whispered before she tucked her face into the crook of his neck and nestled there. Her fingers trailed along the orange and yellow flames that tracked up from his collarbone and covered some of the scars along his neck.

"Yeah?"

"I love you."

He smiled. "I know."

She looked up so suddenly, she knocked his head back against the pipe.

"Ow!"

"What?"

They both spoke at the same time.

Rubbing the back of his head, he grinned. "Did you know you talk in your sleep?"

Kate's mouth dropped open and her face turned beet red. "I do not!"

He burst into laughter, unable to do anything except nod and hold her tightly to prevent her from climbing off his lap.

"I can't believe—how long?" She punched his shoulder when he wouldn't stop laughing.

"Oh…" He was still laughing. "Maybe… September?"

He snorted when she hit his shoulder again. He was a little bit afraid she would hurt her hand if she kept punching him.

"I've been saying 'I love you' in my sleep for over six months, and you didn't say anything?"

Javi grabbed her fist and kissed it. "Who says I didn't say anything?"

She paused, the blush rising in her cheeks again, and smiled shyly. "So… what did you say?"

He kissed her hand again, smoothing it out from a clenched fist. "What do you think I said? You know I love you."

"Yeah?"

He rolled his eyes. "Of course I do. Now, can we get out of here?"

Kate cocked her head to the side and looked at him sympathetically. "That arthritis acting up again?"

She squealed when he pinched her thigh, and she almost fell out of the pipe again. Laughing, Kate scrambled down and went to put on her jeans and check her camera, which was still set up. Javi watched her, thinking of any number of ways he could distract her since he was done with his work for the day and wanted her done, too.

"So what were you coming back to tell me?"

"Oh, that's right." He lowered himself down. "Reed and Sam got married yesterday."

Kate's eyes lit up and she smiled. It was the same smile she got when she captured the exact light she was hoping for or completed a project she was working on. Javi loved all of her, but he especially loved that smile.

"Well," she said with a grin, "how about that?"

Part Twelve:
Two Lovers

CHAPTER THIRTY-TWO

Pomona, California
April 2011

"It's going to be good."

"But what if it isn't?"

"It will be."

"But—"

"Kate," Javi scowled, "why are you being like this? You're one of the least insecure people I know."

Her eyes wandered around the bustling art walk on the second Saturday of April. Her first gallery show would be in two weeks at one of the bigger galleries in the Pomona Arts Colony. Lydia wanted to play up the local angle and had taken care of most of the details, leaving Kate with little to do but worry about the reception of her series of self-portraits taken in Javi's studio over the previous nine months.

"It's important. Really important, and you and Reed and Sam and Vanessa and everyone are going to be here, and because you're all going to be there, all these journalists are going to be there, and —"

"Do you not want everyone to come?" he cut her off. "Say the word and I'll tell everyone to butt out and stay home."

"No!" She turned to him and put a hand on his chest. "That's not it. I want you all there, it's just the expectations. What if it's not as good as everyone expects?"

Javi frowned, pausing to think before he tugged on her arm to start walking again. "Your stuff's good, Kate. Very good. But you never know. You might be right." Kate came to a halt on the sidewalk, but he only grabbed her hand and kept walking past a group of people who waved and nodded at them both. "It's possible the critics aren't going to like it. Or they'll say something nasty. Or just write something rude because they can. That's kind of the way it works sometimes."

She tried pulling away from him, annoyed that he couldn't just make her feel better for once, but he tugged her back to his side and tucked her under his arm. They continued walking through the streets, stopping at the same taco stand as they had their first night together. They sat down on a curb and Javi cracked open her drink and handed it to her. Kate leaned over, kissing his rough cheek before he gave a reluctant smile and started eating.

As frustrating as it was, Kate knew Javi was never going to be a man who told her what she wanted to hear just to reassure her. And she could also admit it was one of the things she loved most about him. When it came to her photography, she trusted his opinion implicitly because she knew he would always tell her the absolute truth.

"Thanks. I'm still nervous, but thanks. I know you're right. I'm just scared."

"You going to stop taking pictures if they hate it?"

"No."

He smiled and leaned over, returning her kiss and playfully nipping at her cheek. "So what does it matter what they say?"

Kate thought about it for a few moments, enjoying the rush of people that sped past them as they sat on the sidewalk.

"You're right."

"I know." He squeezed her hand. "Just keep doing your thing, Katie. Your stuff is real and raw and beautiful. The important people are going to see that."

Kate glanced at him from the corner of her eye, marveling at how easy it was to love him. Most of their friends and family still found Javi and Kate something of an oddity. He was taciturn, antisocial, and old enough that more than one person commented. She was optimistic, friendly, and playful, unless she was in the middle of a shoot.

Yet despite all their differences, Kate and Javi just worked. Dee had seen it. Reed saw it, and even Kate's father had told her the month before he thought Javi was "good for her." Their friends might have been initially stumped, but no one could deny that the two made each other happy; and both were doing exceptional work.

Javi finished his food and stood, holding a hand out to Kate, who ate the last bite of her taco and reached out for him. He tossed their garbage away, put an arm around her, and held her a little closer as they meandered through the crowd. She leaned her head on his shoulder and kept moving forward.

CHAPTER THIRTY-THREE

New York City, New York
September 2011

"Why do I have to keep telling you to hold still?"

The afternoon sun streamed through the windows of their apartment as Sam lay on the bed, propped up by pillows and surrounded by rumpled sheets as her husband of six months perched next to her, sighing in frustration as he tried to work.

"It tickles." She giggled as the paintbrush traced over her stomach. "Maybe you should distract me. Take your clothes off. You being naked always distracts me."

Reed smirked. "I'm sure you'd be plenty distracted, but I don't think you'd be holding still. You never hold still; it's one of the reasons I love you." He winked, and his fingers traced up and around her swollen abdomen. He laid a gentle kiss on her bellybutton before the paintbrush swirled around it in an intricate filigree.

"Whose idea was this again? Oh yes, yours. This was your idea."

"It's a great idea. Be quiet."

"I already have stretch marks down there, don't I?" Sam wrinkled her nose a little as she stared at her pregnant belly. When they found out she was pregnant five months before, she had been surprised, to say the least. They had been told conceiving would be difficult, so she and Reed were initially shocked, then thrilled, when the doctor told them the unexpected news.

They had quietly married in a small ceremony the previous March, six months after they had been reunited in California and two months after they moved back to New York. They'd spent a relaxing week in Savannah for their honeymoon, where Sam painted the oak allée of Forsyth Park, this time including the old men who sat in the park feeding the birds, and the young children playing in front of the fountain. Reed took countless pictures of her as she worked, feeling invigorated by the camera for the first time in years.

Lydia had been thrilled to have them back, though she was less than thrilled when both of them seemed determined to spend several months out of the year in Southern California. Reed and Sam just dug their heels in and told her to deal with it.

"Reed?" Sam asked again. "I have stretch marks, don't I?"

"Mmmhmm," he mumbled, his forehead wrinkled as he traced the elaborate Mehndi designs over his wife's pregnant belly with black tempera paint. "I want to go back to India when the baby's old enough. I miss the colors. Maybe my mom can go with us." He continued tracing. "I should have done this on your hands and feet with henna when we got married. I think Dee did for her wedding."

Sam laughed, but tried to hold still when he shot her a dirty look. "I'm not Indian, Reed," she pointed out logically. "There might have been a few funny looks at the courthouse."

"Who cares? It's beautiful." He drew out the word sensuously as the brush swirled along her skin. "And so are your stretch marks."

"Stretch marks are *not* beautiful."

"They are when they're on my wife who is pregnant with our child. They're pretty great then, if you ask me. Besides... they're interesting," Reed murmured.

His head cocked to the side as he continued painting; and his dark hair, which he had grown out a little, fell into his eyes. "It's your skin, but different. That's what makes it beautiful."

Reed's eyebrows furrowed in concentration as he continued, speaking quietly as the brush moved over and around her belly. "We're always changing. Why do you think I like to photograph people? Every person is unique. Changing all the time. No two pictures are alike." He was silent after that, but finally looked up when he heard her sniff. "Hey, what's wrong?"

Sam brushed the tears away. "I love the way you see people. I love the way you see *me*. I wish more people looked at the world the way you do."

He smiled, pausing to wipe the rest of the tears from the corner of her eye. "Don't cry. Besides, if everyone saw the world the way I did, we'd be poor, because no one would want my pictures." Reed winked at her, and she laughed at his self-deprecation.

"Okay, now hold still." He frowned as he continued his work.

"Don't make me laugh, then."

"This is going to photograph beautifully with this light. I can't wait to see it."

"Black and white?"

"Mmmhmm."

"You're going to want to do this every month, aren't you?"

"Yep. Every single month." He continued swirling paint around her hips as she rolled her eyes. "It's going to be great. Your belly's just going to get bigger and bigger."

"Damn you and your tall genes."

"If you wanted short, stubby babies, you should have married Javi."

"Um, no," she snorted. "And I think Kate might have something to say about that idea."

"Hold still," he ordered again.

"Are you almost finished?"

"Almost." He trailed a few strokes of the brush up toward Sam's recently bountiful breasts. She looked and saw a smile twitching the corners of his mouth.

"Are you photographing those, too?"

"Maybe. Just for posterity, you know."

"Posterity. Right," she said, smiling at him.

Just as Reed was filling in the designs on her left side, she felt a small wave ripple under her skin. Reed gasped, and Sam looked at him.

"What? What is it?"

"The baby moved," he whispered.

"Reed, I told you the baby moves all the time. Especially when I'm lying still."

He smiled in excitement. "But I saw him this time." He folded two long fingers, gently laying the backs against the side of her belly where she'd felt the small undulation. He sat, barely breathing until she felt another small slip of movement against his hand. Reed looked up at her, beaming.

"That's the first time you've felt him, right?"

He set the brush to the side and stretched out next to her on the bed, the paint momentarily forgotten. "Yes." He kissed her tenderly. Reed stroked her cheek, then her hair as he hid his face in her neck. She felt his soft breath against her skin when he whispered, "Not dreaming?"

"Not dreaming." Her hand reached up to lay against his jaw, and she felt the deep rise and fall of his chest pressed against her shoulder.

"I love you," he said, then sat up to finish the paint. "And as soon as these pictures are finished, I'm going to spend a few hours showing you how much."

She laughed before he hushed her again. Sam said, "I can't decide whether you in work mode is sexy or irritating right now."

"I say, go with sexy," he said as his eyebrows furrowed in concentration.

"Of course you do."

Sam smiled when she felt the last cold lick of the brush against her belly; then Reed started cleaning up and arranging the sheets to drape around her before he went to his camera, ducking down to adjust the tripod so he could take his shots.

Her eyes stalked him, handsome and wild in the afternoon light, oblivious to her admiring gaze. He was wearing only a pair of faded jeans. His dark hair was tangled from waking that morning, and he hadn't shaved in days.

Despite their years together, the heartbreak of their separation, and the challenges of their reconciliation, Reed still captured Sam's imagination like no one else in the world, and her fingers itched for her sketchbook. But she relented and lay still, basking as he turned his focus on her. He bent down and adjusted the settings on the camera before he looked through the lens.

"Ah," he said with a slow smile, "there you are."

CHAPTER THIRTY-FOUR

Pomona, California
September 2011

"Lydia's in town next week," Kate said as she read the local paper and drank coffee at the kitchen table of the house in Lincoln Park.

Javi flipped the eggs onto a plate and carried it over, setting it down in the middle of the table and handing her a fork.

"Thanks, baby," she murmured and frowned at the article he'd pointed out to her about a new development that was supposed to be going in adjacent to downtown. "You, know, I don't know how they think this is going to benefit the neighborh—"

"Lydia?" he interrupted, staring at her until she looked up. He reached over to their shared plate and took a bite of sausage. "Did she call you? What does she want? Your stuff or mine?"

"She's angling for the sculpture again. Wants it for a show. She called trying to get me to convince you—"

"Not gonna happen," he bit out, scowling into his coffee. "I'll talk to her. She doesn't need to be bothering you with that shit again. You've got stuff to do."

Kate shrugged and took a bite of the fried eggs. "I can call her. You two will just end up arguing. No need to piss her off unless we have to. I told her you didn't want to show it. It's my fault for showing her the pictures I took in the first place. I'm still kicking myself for that." She shook her head ruefully.

He grunted as he sipped his coffee. "Did she tell you I won't have to shave for those publicity shots she wants Reed to do next month?"

Kate snickered. "I thought your birthday was in May?"

He narrowed his eyes. "Haha. Apparently bad boy artists with tattoos are all the rage in the art world this month. Did you know you were such a lucky woman? She wants to take full advantage of my natural charm. She even wanted me to pierce my ears. That, obviously, was a no."

Kate almost snorted coffee through her nose. "Oh really? Did she ask you to wear skinny jeans, too?" She chuckled in amusement, but didn't miss the embarrassed expression on her boyfriend's face. "She did?" Kate exclaimed, before bursting into laughter.

"That was a no, too."

"Hipster Javi," she said as he glared at her. Kate just grinned as he sat near the windows in the sun. She loved the way the light caught the tiny specks of silver that flecked his hair. She knew Javi hated it, but Kate liked the small signs that marked the passage of their time together.

"I guess I understand why she wants that sculpture. It's the kind of thing reporters eat up."

It was true. After Kate's first big show in May, critics had been as interested in the intriguing relationship between the well-known sculptor and the photographic newcomer as they were in the actual show. Kate and Javi had let Lydia do the talking, trying to stay out of it as much as possible and keep their relationship private.

"I guess it's not *that* big a deal, and if we're going to get technical, I gave you the sculpture, so if you wanted to let Lydia show it in a gallery—"

"Javi! Shut up. You know I'm not going to put it in a gallery if you don't want to show it. It's too personal anyway. Besides, it's not mine, it's… community property."

He smirked. Kate knew he loved pissing her off, just to get a rise out of her.

"Not technically it isn't, unless you've decided to marry me this week."

Kate glanced up before taking another sip of coffee. "You quit smoking yet?"

His eyes narrowed. "Not this week."

Kate raised a single eyebrow. "Let me know when you do." She took another bite of the eggs.

Javi had been cutting back gradually, and even stashed a box of the dreaded nicotine patches in his truck, but he hadn't slapped one on yet because he was still working on the cast for her ring. If he had to give up cigarettes to marry the woman, there was no need to do it prematurely.

He shrugged and decided to change the subject. "I have some other pieces I did in mahogany I'll show her; maybe it'll distract her for a while." He grabbed the paper she wasn't really reading and took another drink of coffee. "How long is she here?"

Kate scowled when she lost the paper, but took a bite of the spicy sausage he had cooked to go with the eggs. "A month or so, I think."

He saw her chew, finally registering when her mouth began to burn. She started breathing a little more heavily and took a drink of coffee. "Did you put hot sauce on these again?" She glared across the table.

He reached over and took another bite, smiling an evil grin. "What? I cook breakfast, I get to make what I like. Lightweight." She stood up, scowling at him and slapping his shoulders which were shaking with laughter. She walked to the sink to get a drink of water, trying to wash the scorch from her mouth. Still laughing, Javi rose from the table and went to stand behind her, boxing her in at the counter as she reached behind to elbow him in the ribs.

"Not funny," she muttered between gulps of water.

He lifted the tangled hair at the back of her neck. She was wearing one of his old black t-shirts, and her pale skin peeked out from the tiny burns that dotted the shoulders. "Sorry, Katie, but it's very funny." He kissed the back of her neck, still chuckling as she swatted at his arms.

Javi finally grabbed her hands and held them tightly in his own as he wrapped his arms around her. He looked down to see their arms entwined, her pale skin against his vividly tattooed forearms. Their hands tangled together, and he looked again at the small letter "K" he had discreetly added to the inside of his wrist. When her arm twisted, he saw the small "J" on the inside of her own, and he felt his heart swell.

He leaned in and lightly bit her neck, right behind her jaw. "I love you," he whispered.

Catching his sudden change of mood, she worked her arms loose, and turned to put them around his neck so she could look in his eyes. "I love you, too," she said before she lay a soft kiss on his lips. "Even if you do try to burn my tongue off."

He nuzzled along her jaw. "Want me to kiss it and make it better?"

"Yes," she said right before his mouth caught hers. He pulled her close, grabbing her waist and turning them so he was leaning against the counter. She pressed against his chest, and he cradled her hips in his strong hands.

Javi finally pulled back and looked into her heated blue eyes with a cocky smile. "Better?"

"Much."

"Hmmm, do we have anything to do today?" he asked as he played with a piece of her wild, red hair.

"Sadly, yes. I need to get some work done for my December show, and then Mari invited us over for dinner with the boys." He grunted when she straightened up. "And didn't you say you wanted to go see that guy in Ontario about some salvage metal? Otherwise, I'd say we needed to catch up on our sleep and hide in the house all weekend."

Javi nicked her neck with his teeth before he walked to the table to finish his coffee. He picked up the breakfast dishes, and put them in the sink as Kate went back to their bedroom to shower and get dressed.

He walked down the hall to their room, reaching down to grab his boots by the door so he could join her at the warehouse while she worked. He stopped at the dresser to get a clean t-shirt and, glancing up, he saw the photograph Reed had taken of them earlier that summer sitting in a simple brown frame.

In typical O'Connor fashion, it didn't show their whole faces, but Reed had positioned Kate so her keen blue eyes lined up with Javi's stubborn jaw. She was looking down toward his collarbone, and the lens captured the swell of her cheek as she began to smile. His chin tilted toward her, and his mouth was slightly open. Kate's eyes were warm and loving as she stared at his scarred neck, and Javi marveled at the way she saw him.

His finger came up to trace the lock of hair in the photograph as it fell forward a little, and he remembered doing the same thing as his other arm wrapped around her back when they took the picture. He heard her hum as she got ready in the bathroom, and his eyes drank in the small traces of her scattered throughout the room.

A camera on the nightstand. A little blue tank top rumpled on the floor. A ponytail holder on the dresser with a few long, red hairs twisted in it.

Javi smiled at the small and welcome intrusions and decided it might be a good day to quit smoking after all.

THE END

ABOUT THE AUTHOR

Elizabeth Hunter is a contemporary fantasy, paranormal romance, and contemporary romance author. She is a graduate of the University of Houston Honors College in the Department of English (Linguistics) and a former English teacher.

She currently lives in Central California with a six-year-old ninja who claims to be her child. She enjoys reading, writing, travel, and bowling (despite the fact that she's not very good at it). Someday, she plans to learn how to scuba-dive. And maybe hangglide. But that looks like a lot of running.

Her contemporary fantasy series, *The Elemental Mysteries*, is a paranormal romance available in e-edition and paperback at all major online retailers. ***A Hidden Fire, This Same Earth,*** and ***The Force of Wind*** are now available. Book Four, ***A Fall of Water,*** will be available in Summer 2012.

Learn more about her writing at ElizabethHunterWrites.com or visit the Elemental Mysteries fan site at ElementalMysteries.com. She may be contacted by e-mail at elizabethhunterwrites@gmail.com. Follow her on twitter at @E__Hunter or on Facebook at her page "Elemental Mysteries by Elizabeth Hunter."

Made in the USA
Lexington, KY
26 February 2014